I0756449

THE WEIGHT OF FORGIVENESS

When her family's long-kept secrets come to light, forgiveness may be more difficult than she ever imagined...

A NOVEL

ELIZABETH RAY

This book is a work of fiction. Any references to historical events, real people (living or deceased), organizations, or places are intended only to provide a sense of authenticity and are used fictitiously. All other characters, dialogue, and incidents are products of the author's imagination, and any resemblance is coincidental and is not to be interpreted as real.

Text copyright © 2025 by Elizabeth Ray

All rights reserved.

Cover design by Rica Graphics

No part of this book may be used or reproduced by any means, graphic, electronic, or mechanical, including photocopying, recording, taping, or by any information storage retrieval system, without the written permission of the publisher, except in brief quotations embodied in critical articles and reviews.

ISBN-13: 979-8-218-59352-0 (paperback)

ISBN-13: 979-8-218-61040-1 (eBook)

First Edition: February 2025. Revised: February 2026.

For Jay,

You are the light of my life.
I love you beyond words.

In loving memory of my father,
Melvin M. Dunn Jr.
You will forever be in our hearts, Chops.
I love you.

THE WEIGHT OF FORGIVENESS

"We cannot change the past, but we can change our attitude toward it. Uproot guilt and plant forgiveness. Tear out arrogance and seed humility. Exchange love for hate—thereby, making the present comfortable and the future promising."

—Maya Angelou

CHAPTER ONE

LOST

Silence. The silence made the darkness unbearable.

Disturbing thoughts of failure crept into the vulnerable spaces in her mind as she anxiously stared at the benevolent Post-it note left on her desk.

Mia,
I hope things are coming along
with your exhibit presentation.
Don't let me down.
- Fred.

Her heart sank into her stomach.

She read between the lines, recognizing subtle hints of disappointment. Negative affirmations began mocking her for the blank presentation form peeking out from under a pile of books on her desk. *You're such a failure. You'll never finish in time.*

Anxiety triggered the darkness. The darkness triggered the deafening silence, trapping her in a familiar prison, with four thick walls surrounding her, painted in a dismal shade of muted black. No escape. No way out. Just silence and darkness. She pressed her hand to her chest, feeling her heart's fast, unsteady beat. It was her only confirmation that she was still alive and the darkness hadn't consumed her yet. Her lungs gasped for the air that her throat now restricted. She leaned forward, pressing her eyelids shut, realizing the four walls were closing in on her. Warm tears streamed down the thick foundation on her cheeks as she braced herself for impact.

A door slammed shut in the hallway and jolted her back to reality. She was shaking. Her head rested on her keyboard as her body slumped over her desk. She lifted herself up. The stiff mechanical keys clicked and popped back into place as she massaged her soft, imprinted cheek. Her espresso-brown foundation was now smudged on the weathered keys. She felt helpless, realizing her unsteady movements had caused unrecognizable words to appear on her computer screen. She had completely ruined all the work she had typed. Taking a moment to regain focus, she thought, *Again? Not again.*

Mia didn't understand why her own thoughts felt so overwhelming. Her anxiety attacks were becoming more frequent and harder to handle. This latest episode stemmed from a simple yellow Post-it note on her desk. Her boss, Mr. Garner, often checked in, leaving subtle messages of encouragement that Mia took as a sign of disappointment. That's all it took. Each time her thoughts constructed scenes of failure, her mind whisked her away into darkness. There was no time to seek refuge.

She peered around the room, breathing in the stale air of her windowless office. The bright fluorescent lights above her pierced her eyes. Her vision was blurry, and her hands were still shaking. She tried to find a distraction within the room, but all she could find were wilting plants and chipped gray paint that disfigured the walls. Mia tried to stand from her chair but felt the weight of anxiety still pressing down on her. She heard a faint knock at the door and turned to see a figure creeping into her office.

"Hey girl," the figure whispered. "Are you okay?"

Mia rubbed her eyes, allowing the blurry figure to come into focus. She was relieved to see Elizabeth, or "Bee", standing by the door. Bee was Mia's closest friend in the world. She was the one person who understood Mia's condition and left judgment out of the way, where it belonged.

"Hey, Bee," Mia muttered, trying to clear her throat. "I'm okay. I had another attack, but I think it's over now. Thanks for checking on me."

"Yeah, of course. I didn't see you at the afternoon meeting. I got worried. I thought you might have fallen asleep after that big lunch we ate. Here, drink this." Bee closed the office door behind her, walking over with a fresh cup of hot coffee. She'd made it just the way Mia loved, with extra sugar and hazelnut creamer poured in. Mia thanked Bee and sipped the hot contents of the thick paper cup. Bee gave her a moment to collect herself before continuing her conversation. No stranger to seeing Mia that way, she thought it best to allow her time after an attack to process everything. The two had met during a stressful semester as juniors at NYU. Bee often held Mia's hand through her frequent stress-induced anxiety attacks. They became as close as sisters after helping one another study and finally graduating together. Mia had never felt such a strong connection before, and Bee appreciated having another girl to bond with. Growing up with five brothers made it hard to find someone she could relate to.

Bee propped herself on the corner of Mia's desk, still waiting for the right moment to speak. Her short, red-and-white plaid skirt lifted higher than expected, and she bounced back down to the floor to avoid Mia getting a glimpse of her underwear. Mia was always getting on Bee about her short skirts and tight tops. Mia's style was more unadventurous and modest, gravitating towards lackluster hues of black and gray. She shifted her attention to Mia's cluttered desk, making subtle movements to throw away the discarded trash scattered around. She noticed Mia hadn't updated her desk calendar in several weeks. Bee leaned over, lifting and pulling the perforated pages to correctly show the month and year of September 2004.

She turned her attention back to Mia, who silently sipped away at her coffee and caught sight of Mia's shifted wig. Her natural hair peeked out from underneath, begging to be cared for. Bee loved Mia's jet-black, kinky, coily hair and wondered why Mia was always putting wigs and weaves in her head. Today's choice was a light brown wig with darkened roots. She wanted to snatch it off Mia's head, but she refused to give in to temptation. Bee's beautiful honey skin tone and small, enticing shape were compliments of her Puerto Rican mother, but sadly, she was burdened with her father's stringy, flat hair. She called it the "Caucasian curse." She loved her friend dearly, but a bitter coil of jealousy tightened in her heart when it came to Mia's natural hair.

Bee reached over to open Mia's drawer, pulled out a thick wooden paddle brush, and some bobby pins to fix the mess. She carefully pulled off Mia's wig and quickly began re-braiding her hair before someone, like Mr. Garner, barged into the room.

"I don't know," Mia finally whispered. "I feel like crap. I keep having these attacks back-to-back. This deadline is stressing me out." Mia looked back at Bee, who was busy putting a few thick cornrows in Mia's head. Bee mushed the side of Mia's face, telling her to keep her head facing forward.

"He left me another sticky note while we were at lunch," Mia said, keeping her head still.

"What did it say?"

"He tried to be nice this time, but I could feel the disappointment behind it. He said, 'Don't let me down,' like he's already expecting me to fail. He hates me."

"Mr. Garner doesn't hate you," Bee said reassuringly. "He hired you because he saw the great work you did for the exhibits at that art expo last summer. He wants you to do your best, that's all."

"I mean, I finally have the chance to work with you every day. You'd think I'd be happy." Mia paused. "I'm supposed to be happy, right?"

"I'm not the one you should be convincing," Bee said with a look of concern.

Mia sighed. "I can't seem to figure out an idea for this project. Why is this so difficult for me? I've never had this type of creative block before." Mia lifted a stack of papers, pulled a monogrammed coaster from underneath the pile, and put her coffee cup down to rest. She placed her head in her warmed hands and felt the urge to scream.

Weeks earlier, Mia had taken a chance to work alongside Bee at a new museum in the Bronx. They were tasked with creating exciting, "unsaturated" Black History Month exhibits alongside a handful of other curators. Everyone had to present their idea for the grand opening in February, just a few months away. Despite her academic achievements and artistic ability to design award-winning exhibits, it had taken her weeks to come up with absolutely nothing to present to her boss. She couldn't think of a single useful idea for the project. Everything she researched and built as a suitable foundation for a collection was thrown out. Her ideas didn't fit what Mr. Garner was looking for. If Mia came to their next staff meeting empty-handed again, she'd be out of a job.

Although seemingly unaware of the reason, she knew the exact source of her trouble. A terrible feeling festered within her, surfacing for air. She couldn't ignore it anymore. Mia had gotten by in life without having to face how totally disconnected she was from her melanated heritage. It was difficult for her to find a connection with other Black people. She knew she was a black woman, but had nothing to show for it up to that point.

For most of her life, Mia had been sheltered, living in a predominantly White neighborhood. Her upbringing, no fault of her own, was now working against her. The way she spoke, dressed, and other whitewashed characteristics placed a permanent target on her back. The frequent teasing for her preppy white girl tendencies had become routine. She wanted to love her culture, but she would always revert to what she knew. The push and pull made her dizzy. Rather than being proud of who she was and embracing her individuality, she felt awkward, introverted, and cast out.

Mia pressed her back into the support cushion of her office chair; she was determined to steer clear of her mental prison. Bee yearned to give Mia what she needed. Knowing that words were insufficient, she bent down and hugged Mia from behind.

"You've got a lot on your plate, Mia. It makes sense why you're feeling this way."

"Everyone in the office, including you, has an exhibit idea to present next week, and I don't. I can't think of anything interesting to hand in. Maybe deciding to come work here with you was a mistake."

"That's because all you did was…" Bee laughed under her breath but stopped herself, careful not to hurt Mia's feelings.

"Go ahead. You can say it. All I did was curate exhibits for and about white people."

"Well, you said it, not me." Bee chuckled. "That Rosa Bonheur collection you put together a while back was amazing, though!" Bee again cut her humor short, noticing that Mia remained unamused and silent. She cleared her throat and tried to find a way to comfort her friend again.

"Look, why don't I come over tonight and we'll brainstorm?"

"We never get to brainstorming," Mia groaned. "We just pop open a bottle of wine and spend the night talking or watching some dumb movie. You know, doing the exact opposite of what we planned."

"Well, at least we have fun!" said Bee. "There, I'm all done. You're back to looking normal now!" Bee handed Mia a small mirror from her drawer. Mia smiled, feeling a little less disheveled.

"Well, if we don't get to brainstorming ideas for the project, we can at least start thinking of what to do for my birthday coming up," said Bee as she flipped through Mia's calendar to ensure her birthday was circled. "I know you're not as excited as I am about turning twenty-three this year, but everything is going to get better, Mia. My spiritual numbers book says twenty-three means we're on the right path and there's personal growth and transformation ahead!"

"Don't let it turn into another complaint about me not having a birthday party this year. I swear I don't know what fun you think I'm supposed to have when it's cold outside."

"It's never too cold to party!" Bee waved her arms in the air, dancing and bumping Mia.

Mia laughed, bumping Bee back.

The two continued their conversation, with Bee hoping that changing the subject would help Mia out of her depressed mood.

A few moments later, there was a knock at the door. Mia instructed the visitor to come in. Yvonne, the museum's receptionist, dubbed the office *mother* for her plump figure, loving nature, and amazing cooking abilities, stood in the doorway with a somber look. Mia and Bee welcomed Yvonne with a smile. Noticing her distorted expression, the two women became worried.

"Is everything okay, Yvonne?" Bee asked.

"Someone called wanting to speak to you, Mia," replied Yvonne.

"Did you take a message?"

"Yes, I did." Yvonne paused. "I'm not sure I want to tell you like this, though." She walked closer to the desk and slid a piece of paper with a phone number on it to Mia.

"A lawyer, Mr. Lucas, called. Here is his number. He will explain everything to you."

"Lawyer? Wait, what do you mean, lawyer? What happened, Yvonne? Did he tell you?"

"Yes, but—"

"Just tell me. It's okay."

"I told him you were busy and would call him back, but he told me anyway. He said..." Yvonne's voice cracked under pressure. She tried again to get out what she needed to say, this time blurting it out.

"Mia, I'm so sorry to have to tell you this, but he said your father passed away, and your presence is requested at the lawyer's office to handle some legal matters."

Mia sat frozen, staring at Yvonne. The news stunned her, but for the wrong reason. Mia looked up at Bee, who was also standing there speechless. Bee looked down with puzzled eyes.

"Mia, didn't your father—"

"Yeah..." Mia muttered. She grabbed her desk phone and dialed the number on the paper but was greeted by a voicemail. Mia left a quick message with her phone number and the best time to call. Slamming the phone down, she grabbed her purse from behind her chair and walked past Bee and Yvonne.

"Mia, are you okay?" Yvonne asked.

Mia turned around and looked back at Yvonne.

"I appreciate your delivering the message, but I have to go."

"My condolences to you and your family," Yvonne said, suppressing her empathetic tears.

"No need." Mia shook her head in disbelief, letting out a sarcastic chuckle. "My father is supposed to be dead already. He died before I was born."

Mia made her way to the parking lot, still in a state of shock. She pushed her thoughts of failure aside, making room for a new problem to trouble her mind. Mia rolled her eyes and quickly backed out of her parking space. She needed the truth, but it was hidden behind the one door she had vowed never to knock on again.

CHAPTER TWO

NORMA

Mia sat in silence the entire trip. She normally enjoyed the chance to travel outside the city. Taking in the beautiful scenic views always calmed her. It was a pleasant escape from her usual environment of brick high-rises and rusted train tracks. Today was different. Even though it was a clear, beautiful fall day, she hadn't noticed a single fall color-coated tree or any of the normal landmarks she used as guides. No music to pass the time and no wandering, happy thoughts. Rather, she replayed painful parts of her past as she sped up the highway in her old forest green '92 Honda.

From the moment of conception, Mia's fate had been sealed by the careless decisions of two intoxicated strangers. One passionate night left her mother, Norma, pregnant. What briefly resembled a promising relationship collapsed into misery with the sudden news of her lover's unexpected death. That was the truth into which Mia was born. Her world began on a foundation of division.

When Mia was younger, she discovered her mother's diary. Most of its pages had been torn out. What remained revealed fragments of Norma's inner life, including the truth that she had never planned to become a mother. Norma wrote about her childhood—about a carefree spirit shaped by ambition and a longing to become a great American female lawyer. She admired women like Sandra Day O'Connor and Jane Bolin, hoping one day her name could be as eminent as theirs. Life, however, intervened, and Norma Briggs became the one thing she never wanted to be: tied down. Forced to abandon her dream, she settled into a semi-satisfying career as a teacher, lecturing students on politics and law instead of practicing them herself.

Norma's shame hardened into the cold, unyielding childhood Mia remembered. Their relationship had been turbulent from the beginning. They simply did not know how to coexist. She lacked the warmth of a loving mother, leaving Mia untouched by what love was meant to feel like—no hugs, no kisses, no shared moments, no emotional reassurance. In their place were strict rules, relentless academic expectations, and an unspoken agreement to stay out of her mother's way.

Mia yearned to discover who her father was for as long as she could remember. She knew that Norma herself had been adopted; her parents had died when she was still a baby, leaving her to grow up in foster care. Mia never felt compelled to search for anyone from her mother's side. She believed that anyone related to Norma, besides herself, would be the same—cold, distant, unreachable. Yet Mia felt an undeniable pull toward her father and his family, a quiet, persistent curiosity that refused to fade. Norma was the only family she had ever known, and Mia often wondered whether family was even the right word for what bound them together.

Mia searched relentlessly for traces of her father and his family. She waited until Norma left the house before rifling through locked drawers and hidden belongings. She listened outside closed doors, straining to catch fragments of guarded phone calls. Aside from the diary, every attempt led nowhere. She longed for proof she was not alone—that, like everyone else, she had a family: cousins to play with and trade fashion tips; aunts to teach her how to properly apply makeup and warn her not to kiss boys; uncles who drank too much and burned burgers on hot Sunday afternoons. Yet each search brought her no closer to the truth. It was as though Norma had deliberately erased her past. Whenever Mia asked about her father or his family, she was met with resistance and icy silence. What she wanted, more than answers, was what she had always been missing—family and love.

After Mia moved out to attend college, Norma decided she'd done her job as a mother and moved to a more comfortable home upstate. From that time until now, Mia had scarcely seen her mother. Her last trip to see Norma ended in a heated argument after Mia tried to talk about the emptiness she felt and how she wanted them to go to therapy together to work out their differences. Norma brushed her feelings off, saying, "I can't change the past, Mia. You need to grow up and move on." Mia hadn't spoken to her mother since, but she was the only one who could explain Mr. Lucas' call. She vowed not to leave without answers.

After hours of reliving painful memories and regurgitating hurt, she pulled into the driveway of her mother's small, cottage-style home. The home's grayish-blue paint her mother had chosen made Mia want to vomit every time she saw it. The dreary exterior perfectly matched its solemn occupant.

Mia sat in the car for a while, watching the calico-colored clouds lose their once vibrant hue as the sun retired behind the multicolored houses in the neighborhood. The Honda began to sputter and shake, signaling to Mia that she'd been idling for too long. Taking a few slow breaths, she turned off the engine, opened the door, and forced herself toward the door. After a few hard knocks, a voice barked from inside.

"Who the hell is it?"

"Open the door, Mother," Mia replied.

There was a moment of silence. The lock turned, and Mia was met with glaring eyes and a familiar frown. The smell of stale cigarettes hit her instantly, and she gagged at the overwhelming stench. Norma stood there in her favorite maroon bathrobe, with her thinning hair wrapped in a matching silk bonnet. Her skin looked ashy and neglected. What had once been a statuesque figure was now overweight and uneven, her stomach folds brushing against the doorframe. Norma didn't know why her daughter was there, but neither woman had any interest in pleasantries.

"What in the world are you doing here, Mia? And why do you have that ridiculous wig on your head? I wish you would take—"

Interrupting her mother's usual rant about her hairstyle, Mia pushed past her and into the house. Her ballet flats slapped against the wooden floor of the dark, hollow foyer as she hurried toward the living room. She cringed. The dreary grayish-blue paint had crept in, smothering the once-tranquil tan walls. The reek of stale cigarettes thickened as she entered, clinging to her throat and making her stomach turn. Ashtrays overflowed with damp ashes and crushed filters, scattered carelessly throughout the room. Ember-scarred holes peppered the carpet, which felt spongy and worn beneath her feet. Several neglected houseplants strained toward the bay window, their brittle leaves reaching for warmth that never came. Mia chose to overlook the concerning condition of her mother's home and moved to the center of the room to confront Norma.

"Who is he?" Mia yelled. "Who is my father? You told me he died before I was born, but that can't be true. I got a call today at work that he *just* died. Norma, tell me what's going on!"

All the emotion drained from Norma's face as she collapsed onto the deep, cold cushions of the black leather couch behind her. Mia watched her expressions shift from confusion to sadness. Norma wrapped her arms around herself, pulling at her bathrobe while tears began to part ways from her puffy eyes. Mia had never seen her mother cry. Overwhelmed, Mia sank into the matching loveseat across from her.

"He finally *died*?" Norma whispered, "I can't believe it."

Mia stared at her, as fury rose up inside her.

"He *finally* died?! What do you mean, he *finally* died? He's already supposed to be dead, Norma!"

"Stop yelling at me, Mia. I know you're upset, but have some respect for your mother!"

"I have nothing for you, Norma, after how you treated me the last time I was here. It's taking all the patience I have to even look at you right now. You've always told me I had no family. You forced me to look to you for everything—a father, a grandparent, a sibling, or anybody else I would consider family. So, tell me—who is he?"

Mia felt her eyes water. She sat there looking at her mother, waiting for an answer. Norma sat frozen, staring at the floor. She was ashamed, unsure of how to tell Mia the truth. Silence stretched between them until Norma reached for a cigarette on the end table.

"I know you won't believe me, but I didn't do this to hurt you," she said, lighting the cigarette.

"Who. Is. He?" Mia repeated sternly.

"Your father's name was David. You never knew about him because—" Norma paused, drawing in a breath. "Because I didn't tell him about you until it was too late."

"Go on," she demanded. Norma leaned back heavily into the couch. She stared at the floor, cleared her throat, and stubbed out the half-burned cigarette.

"I'm not thrilled about telling you any of this," she said. "But since he's gone now—and you're so determined to know—I won't hide the truth from you anymore."

"I remember it was the summer of 1980. I was out with some friends, celebrating our acceptance into law school. We worked our asses off, and we wanted to have some well-deserved fun. I was on top of the world. I aced my LSAT, and I'd planned the next few years of my life out, step by step, to get to my goal. I couldn't think of anything more thrilling than becoming a lawyer. I remember putting on my favorite black and white polka-dot dress that night. I even sewed in some shoulder pads to make me look a little classier. We walked into some little rinky-dink bar to start the night off, and that's when I saw him. He was behind the bar working, oblivious to the hole I was staring into his muscular chest. Damn, I can still see him standing there now. I walked over to an empty stool and asked him for a Sex on the Beach. He smiled at my obvious attempt at making a pass at him.

"I don't remember much of what we talked about, what I drank, or what dumb things I must've whispered in his ears. All I really remember is him. Everything about him. David. He was tall and handsome, with these brown eyes that could've stopped a woman in her tracks. Well, at least they stopped me in mine. He smelled like a fresh bar of shea butter soap, and his thick, black beard was oiled and freshly trimmed. His skin was smooth, chocolate brown, and covered with random tattoos and intentional muscles. It only took a few moments, but I was positive I was in love. That love that Marvin and Patti sang about. I'd never been in love before. It was an amazing and terrifying feeling: that strong, that quick. I was sure we were going to be together forever—no mistake about it. We spent the night laughing and throwing back shots of everything we could get our hands on.

"I've never told anyone about what really happened, but I guess I have no reason to hide it anymore. That night was the best night of my life. I had flings before. Men who thought they knew what they were doing. Thought they knew how to please me, but nothing ever felt as good as David. I still can't believe it because it was only one night. My friends

went on with their night, leaving me to the mercy of his love. Somehow, someway, we made it to a hotel across the street together. His hands acted as if they felt me before. Like they knew exactly what I needed and where to go to give it to me, his kisses left absolutely nothing to be desired. We went on and on all night until I finally passed out.

"I remember waking up to this one beam of light shining in my face. The sun was up and so was I. I wanted more. I wanted to taste his gin-soaked lips again. I wanted him to wrap his fingers around the roots of my hair and sink his body into mine. I reached over to find him. To feel him again. All I felt were empty sheets and a piece of paper where his perfect body once lay. It said everything he was too nervous to tell me the night before. How great it was for him. How he had a great time. How funny and beautiful I was. He went on to say he was married and how he couldn't leave his wife. How he made a wonderful and fantastic mistake. How he'd never forget me. How he was sorry for any pain he caused, but he had to leave.

"I must've cried for hours. I wasn't going to stop or find the strength to want to leave the room, but the housekeeping lady came to the door, so I had no choice but to leave. David left me a cab fare with his note. That was it. I made my way home, crying for days after that. In less than twenty-four hours, I found out what love and depression felt like. Both emotions fought endlessly to suppress one another. I never felt so helpless before in my whole life.

"Then, a few weeks later, while I was trying my best to recover and move on with my life, I started throwing up and feeling like pure hell. I couldn't get it together. I honestly thought I had the flu. Maybe I was dying from the pain; hell, I didn't know. I went to see a doctor, and sure enough, I got the news that I was going to be a mother. A mother. What did I know about being a mother? A single mother at that. I didn't want to be a single mother. I wanted David. If I was going to be a mother, at least let it be with him by my side.

"Then I got this delusional idea in my head that gave me an ounce of hope. I started thinking, what if David loved me too, and being pregnant would be the driving force he needed to leave his marriage and be with me? What if that was all he needed? What if he was waiting for me? I had to find him and be happy again. So, as soon as I left the doctor's office, I made my way to the bar where we'd met. I honestly hadn't gone back or set foot on that block in fear of seeing him. I wasn't sure if I would kill him or make a fool of myself by getting down on my knees and begging him to feed my addiction for his touch.

"I stepped into the bar, nervous and scared but hopeful. I asked around and learned that David had moved back home to Virginia with his wife to help care for his mother. He didn't leave an address where he'd be. He didn't leave any letters or an indication that he ever wanted to see me again. That was it. I decided to keep everything that happened between David and me to myself. Staying silent was easier than telling the truth. I gave up trying to find him, and I went on to raise you all by myself.

"It wasn't until you were about to graduate from grad school last year that I thought about finding David and telling him you existed. I tried my best to forget about him and leave that one night in the past. I did some searching, but always came up empty-handed. So, I turned to a private investigator for help. They found him after a few weeks and a ton of my money. I went to the address they gave me, which was a hospital in Virginia. I never expected to see him that way after all those years. Propped up in a hospital bed. He had prostate cancer and wasn't sure how long it was going to be before he died. Seeing him that way broke my heart and put me right back to the emptiness I felt when he first left.

Mia abruptly interrupted Norma's story.

"Did you tell him?" she muttered, wiping her tear-stained cheeks. "Did you tell him about me?"

"Yes, but he told me not to tell you we'd met. He was dying, and he decided that it was best to keep the lie going for everyone since he may not live much longer."

"Why didn't he at least try to talk to me? Why didn't he care?"

"He did care, Mia. He asked for every baby picture and every achievement you'd made. Anything he could get his hands on about you, he wanted."

It took Mia a moment to take it all in. Norma was going in, rewriting her entire history. She tried to sift through the emotions now flooding her mind, landing on the only feasible reaction. Anger.

"You've been lying to me since day one. You knew how much I needed a father. You knew how much I needed a family. How can you be so heartless?"

"Mia, I did what was best for you. You have to understand that."

Mia couldn't bear to look at her mother anymore. She sprang to her feet and made her way to the front door. Norma stood up but remained silent. Chasing after Mia would do more harm than good. She had always known this day would come, but having it here now, staring her in the face, was more than she could handle. Even though her actions never revealed it, she did, in fact, love Mia, but the pain of how they came to be together was too much to bear. She had buried her heart and all emotions. Everything she did, she did for Mia, but after years of resentment, fights, and distance, the two women were far from agreeing on anything.

Norma had poured out her pain, hopeful that Mia would respond with understanding and forgiveness, but it was too late. She watched silently as her heartbroken daughter opened the front door and slammed it shut, driving off into the cool fall night.

CHAPTER THREE

TRIGGERED

Mia felt overwhelmed by the words her mother had carelessly used to cut her. Every breath she'd taken from the moment she closed the door behind her was long and arduous. She felt her chest caving in. What she once believed was the truth was only a lie.

Mia made her way back to her small studio apartment in the city and immediately called Bee, frantic for someone to come and help her process what had happened. Within the hour, Bee was by Mia's side.

"It's like I've lost him twice," Mia cried out. "I've lost someone I've never seen. That's the crazy part. Like I've *never* seen this man a day in my life, and I'm sitting here crying over him like he was my best friend."

Bee wrapped her arms around her distraught friend. She remained silent, knowing that nothing she could say would erase the pain Mia was feeling. An hour passed, then another, and another, until the tears subsided. They curled up with blankets on Mia's large sectional couch and fell asleep.

Mia awoke the next morning to find herself covered in used tissues, with Bee snoring on the other side of the couch. She pushed herself up from the burlap-textured cushions. The large analog clock on her purple-painted accent wall told her she was late for work. She nudged Bee and greeted her opening eyes with a frown.

"Bee, I'm so sorry. It's after nine a.m. I didn't mean to keep you up all night and make you late for work. I feel terrible."

Bee smiled and leaned over to pat Mia on the leg.

"Girl, it's okay! I woke up about an hour ago while you were still sleeping and called the office. I let Yvonne know you weren't feeling well, and you wouldn't be in today. I'm going to clock in later this afternoon since I'm supposed to be here to help you get better. I asked her to tell Mr. Garner it was probably that crappy breakroom food you ate!" Bee made Mia giggle as she gestured her disgust, gagging with her finger in her mouth.

"Thanks, Bee. I'll call later and tell them I'll be out for a few days. I don't think I would be much use to anyone right now. Besides, trying to explain this whole situation is weird… like saying, 'Hey, my dead dad just died, so I won't be in for a while.' Nope, I'd rather stick with the 'I'm sick' story." Mia laid her head back down on the arm of the couch.

"Yeah, I agree." Bee stood up, pulling and adjusting the oversized Spice Girls t-shirt she wore to bed. Wiping the dried sleep from her eyes, she walked into the kitchen to make the two some breakfast. She began rummaging through Mia's empty cabinets, opening and closing the wooden drawers, looking for something to eat.

"When do you see the lawyer?"

"Mr. Lucas called while I was at Norma's. He left a message that it's the day after tomorrow and, just my luck, it's in Virginia. I haven't been down there in years. I was thinking about taking the bus, but I'm going to have to drive."

"Do you want me to ride with you?"

"No, you've already done more than enough by just being here. I'll have to ride this one out alone."

Mia had forgotten to wrap her hair, causing all of her cornrows to unravel while she slept. She tossed her head back to keep her hair out of her face and tied her favorite zebra-print scarf around her head. She grabbed a hair tie from the coffee table and pulled the unmanageable hair back into a puffy ponytail.

"This project at work, my father dying twice now, and my worthless mother…it's all too much. I'm surprised I haven't pulled all my hair out!"

"I would much rather you cut it off and give it to me!" joked Bee.

"You can have it. Means nothing to me anyway."

Bee sighed and decided it was now or never to bring up work and the lingering discussion of the exhibit meeting next week. She understood Mia felt depressed about everything going on, but also knew Mia would let her procrastination build up like an aggressive ant hill. She couldn't allow her to go out like that. She loved her friend dearly, and one thing she knew about love was it didn't fear accountability.

"So, do you want to talk about the project before you go to Virginia? We have to talk about it sometime. I hate that it still has to be a topic of conversation."

"Not much to talk about. I don't have anything remotely interesting to showcase for the exhibit. Mr. Garner's going to kill me. I mean, I've never really dug deep into Black history. I guess it never mattered to me. I mean, Norma taught me about Black lawyers, but everything else was 'overused,' as Mr. Garner would say. I got the usual MLK, Rosa Parks, and Malcolm X stories, and I thought that was enough. Like, how did you even come up with *African Americans in Space* for your exhibit idea? I don't even know who Mark Anderson is."

"Not Mark. His name was Michael Anderson, and that's the whole point of the exhibits. To teach these inner-city kids about influential

Black people other than Martin Luther King. There are so many others out there."

"I'm so dumb. You aren't even black, and you know more about black people than I do."

"You don't have to be black to know about Black history. One of the professors of African Studies at NYU was an Asian man, remember?"

"Oh yeah, you're right. I think his name was Mr. Nguyen."

"See! Trust me, you're not dumb...you just have 'blonde' moments. We'll think of something for you. We still have a week and a half. Meanwhile, go take care of everything in Virginia, come back, and we'll get right to work. No wine, movies, or talks about that cute janitor. We actually work!"

"Sounds like a plan." Mia smiled.

Bee nodded her head and went back to foraging through Mia's cabinets and refrigerator for something to make the two for breakfast. She finally found some Pop-Tarts, three reasonably fresh-looking eggs, and some frozen sausage and got to work making them edible. Just then, Mia jumped up from the couch, startling Bee.

"Oh, my God!" Mia screamed.

"What? What's wrong?"

"Bee, oh my God! I just thought about it," Mia began pacing the floor and waving her hands, trying to convey her discovery. "What if...what if...what if I have family members there in Virginia? What if I have a *family*?"

"Oh yeah! We didn't even think about that!" Bee yelped with excitement.

"I might have aunts and uncles. What if I have some brothers and sisters, too!" Mia jumped up and finally felt a rush of happiness she hadn't felt in a long time.

The two chatted away for the rest of the morning until Bee said her goodbyes and headed to work. Mia made her way to her bedroom and began happily packing for the trip to Virginia.

CHAPTER FOUR

ANTICIPATION

Mia paced the cold ceramic tile floor of her apartment as time crept forward. She couldn't sleep. She could barely eat. Her only source of real nourishment was the prospect of family. It tasted sweeter than anything she'd ever eaten. Happiness was present, but so was fear. She pushed everything aside, including the exhibit presentation deadline and her implacable feelings for Norma. Hours were spent staring out of her eighth-floor window, impatiently watching strangers move along the congested streets and trash-laced sidewalks with purpose.

Just as she felt she was losing her mind, the long-awaited day arrived. Before the alarm could be dismissed, she was up, showering, applying her makeup, and pressing jagged bobby pins into her hair to secure her wig. She shoved a few extra items into her weekender bag and hastily made her way out the door.

She started the old Honda, watching exhaust smoke bloom in the rearview mirror before thinning into the chilly morning air. The "green blob" rattled beneath her like a tired animal, stubborn but reliable. Mia hated driving long distances in it. Every vibration reminded her of its age, and how easily it could fail—but she trusted it anyway. The car had always carried her where she needed to go, even when nothing else had.

Before pulling out of the parking space, she ran through her mental checklist, more out of habit than necessity. The weekender bag and her long brown crossbody purse sat on the passenger-side floor, and a thick packet of MapQuest directions rested beside her bulky, trapper-keeper-style CD binder filled with an eclectic array of music.

She flipped through the binder sleeves, her fingers grazing familiar album covers, each tied to a different version of herself. Choosing the first CD felt strangely important, as if the wrong song might derail the entire trip. Before she could decide, her phone buzzed sharply from inside her purse, the sound jarring enough to make her flinch.

She already knew who it was.

Digging through the purse confirmed it as Norma's name glowed on the screen. Again. Norma had been calling nonstop since Mia stormed off, her persistence as suffocating as it had always been. Mia stared at the phone, her chest tightening. The thought of hearing her mother's voice—dismissive and laced with obnoxious authority—made her stomach churn. She pressed *ignore*, then did it again when the screen lit up moments later. She had nothing left to say.

Every knot she carried inside herself seemed to trace back to Norma. The anxiety. The constant feeling of being out of place, like she was always playing a role she hadn't auditioned for. Even now, alone in the car, she felt watched and judged. With a sharp final motion, Mia powered the phone off. Silence filled the car, fragile but welcome. She clung instead to the thought of Virginia—to the possibility someone there might be searching for her just as desperately as she was searching for them.

The hours slipped by as Mia and her '92 Honda hummed steadily up and down the highway. The passenger seat became cluttered with discarded CDs, each one a small attempt to outrun her thoughts. The music jumped from country to alternative rock before settling into her favorite pop mix—bright voices and polished beats that provided a welcoming distraction. She sang along when she could, and danced in her seat, just enough to feel alive.

When she rolled down the window for fresh air, the wind rushed in, cold and sharp. A few strands of her natural hair slipped loose and whipped against her cheek. Her body tensed as she reached up, fingers moving quickly, tucking the strands back beneath the edges of her wig. The relief was brief. Shameful, familiar voices from her childhood began popping into her head, the ones she always heard when her hair annoyed her.

"Mia's got KINK-O-LINK hair!!"

"Nice Jerry Curl, Mia!"

"Bet she can't even get a comb through that mess!"

Mia tightened her grip on the steering wheel and turned the music up louder to drown out the voices. The road stretched ahead of her, long and uncertain. After a few stops for coffee and doughnuts, she found herself in Richmond, Virginia. She had made it with only minutes to spare.

She pulled into an empty parking space and scanned the lot for anyone entering the tall, solitary brick building. The lot held only a few parked vehicles, with zero movement coming or going into the building. Turning off the car, she pulled down the vanity mirror to examine her appearance. She wanted to look her best. Mia had even gone out and bought a new wig for the occasion, keeping things professional. The brown-bobbed wig she'd chosen complemented her slender, oval-shaped face. Praying for strength, she held back tears of mixed emotions. She emerged from her car, wiped the scattered doughnut crumbs from her lap, and walked with a steady gait into the building.

At first glance, the office lobby was empty, with only a few oddly shaped deco chairs and crumpled magazines spread out on a small gold-painted coffee table. Mia looked around at the bare gray walls that reminded her of her windowless office back home. The office smelled of old library books and burned coffee. She headed to the receptionist's desk on the opposite side of the room and gently tapped the shiny silver call bell at the edge of the counter. Mia smiled at the pretty young woman who emerged from the back office. She wore a boldly chosen yellow-and-black printed blazer, with matching trousers and black high heels that tapped loudly on the concrete floor beneath them. Her hair was braided into an oversized bun atop her head. Her clear chocolate skin and flawless smile were equally impressive, and Mia stared at her.

"He…hello," Mia awkwardly muttered. "I'm Mia Briggs. I'm here to see—"

"Oh, you're Mia Briggs! I'm so glad to see you. I'm Phyllis, Mr. Lucas' assistant. I'm glad you're here, but is something wrong with your cell phone? Mr. Lucas told me it's your best contact, but it's going straight to voicemail. I've been trying to reach you for the past two hours."

Mia suddenly remembered that she had forgotten to turn her phone back on that morning. *Damn you, Norma!* Mia scolded as she once again found something to blame on her mother.

"I'm so sorry," she blurted out. "I turned my phone off and didn't get a chance to turn it back on." Mia began rummaging through her purse again to locate the phone.

"No worries," Phyllis said. "I was only calling to let you know we're running behind and getting started later than expected. We already had lunch. Now, there are some private legal matters that the family must handle, and then we'll call you in. Please wait in the lobby, and I'll let you know when they're ready for you."

"To be honest," said Mia, "I'm not entirely sure why I'm here if all the *family* legal matters are being handled without me in there."

"I'm not sure if Mr. Lucas wants me to go over that with you right now, Miss. Briggs, but I can promise you that your presence was requested." Phyllis came from behind the desk and ushered Mia into the lobby, handing her a crumpled magazine. Her heels tapped loudly as she returned to the desk to continue her work.

Mia thanked Phyllis and resumed her search for her phone. Digging to the bottom of the bag, bypassing several candy wrappers and old makeup sponges, the device came into view. She used her sleeve to wipe away the crumbs and hair that had accumulated on the screen and powered it back on. Voicemails and text messages began dinging for her attention. Skimming through the text messages first, she saw some were from co-workers and one from Bee.

Did you call out today? Mr. Garner came by my office looking for you! Call me!

Mia threw her head back in the chair, smacking her forehead with frustration. She'd forgotten to call Mr. Garner to let him know she'd be out of work again today. Her upcoming due date for her exhibit presentation idea and everything else that was once important to her were now catching fire on the back burner. She raced to find Mr. Garner's number in her contacts, but was cut off by an incoming call. The color rushed from her face as she saw it was Mr. Garner calling. Her heart sank, and she jumped up from the seat and signaled to Phyllis that she'd take the call outside.

"Good afternoon, Mr. Gar—"

"Mia Briggs! Finally! I've been calling you all morning!" Mia cringed at the sound of discontent in his deep voice.

"My apologies, sir. I completely forgot to contact you and let you know I'd be out of the office again today."

"Yvonne told me you were sick. Is everything okay?"

"Yes, I'm doing much better. I may need another day to make sure I'm back to my normal self." Mia paused, hoping that he'd approve.

"Well, she also told me about the phone call you received the other day and how you stormed out of the office. Then you had Elizabeth call in sick for you the next day, and no one has seen you since. Why am I getting the feeling this isn't about you being *sick*, Mia?"

Mr. Garner obviously had a mound of evidence to support his apprehensions. Mia knew she had to come clean. She found a quiet spot outside the office building and pressed her back to the brick wall, searching for the right words that would keep her employed and out of more trouble than she was already in. All she could muster up at first were several sincere apologies for keeping him out of the loop. Then came the preposterous truth. Starting with the message Yvonne gave her, to her unforeseen trip to Virginia, Mia let it all out, begging him to understand that she hadn't wanted to lie, but the situation was so bizarre she didn't think he'd believe her. It was like something out of a work of fiction.

She paused for his reaction. Mr. Garner was an agreeable man. His tall, stout exterior commanded respect around the office, but everyone knew he had an easygoing soul. Unfortunately, his good side was wearing thin after all of her rejected ideas and lack of communication. After a few moments of silence, she heard him clear his throat to speak.

"You have no reason to keep things from me, Mia. I would've understood and been more than forgiving if you had told me the truth. Our presentation meeting is next week. You're free to take as much time as you need until that Friday. However, issues or no issues, I expect to see you in that meeting at nine a.m. sharp, with your exhibit proposal ready for review. If you do not, I will reassign you to Yvonne's position after she retires next month. The choice is yours."

With that, Mr. Garner said goodbye and hung up. Mia returned to the building lobby. She sat down and stared blankly ahead, searching for a way to blame her actions on Norma again, but she knew she was solely to blame. Tears welled in the corners of her eyes. She wiped them away with her sleeve. Mia then felt a tap on her shoulder. It was Phyllis. She handed Mia a tissue and smiled.

"They're ready for you now," she whispered, pointing to the hallway. "Last door on the left."

Mia thanked her for the tissue and headed down the narrow hallway, shaking every step of the way.

CHAPTER FIVE

DAVID

Mia grasped the cold metal doorknob. Her body tensed as she played out scenarios like an old movie reel of what might happen. As much as she wanted to know what was behind the door, she couldn't bring herself to open it. Minutes passed as she stood frozen in fear. Suddenly, the door flew open, and a tall, slender man with curly black hair bumped right into Mia.

"Oh, my!" the man gasped with surprise, brushing his freshly pressed suit and checking for any makeup marks smudged on his chest from the collision. "My apologies, you must be Mia."

"Yes," she croaked.

The man stepped out and closed the door behind him.

"I'm Mr. Lucas. Nice to meet you. We've finished up what we needed to do." He paused, noticing her puffy eyes and face. "Is everything okay?"

"I'm fine," she assured him, still dabbing at her eyes with the crumpled tissue.

"I actually wanted to speak to you before you came in. Unfortunately, your father, David, left it up to me to advise his family about you. You'll have to excuse everyone, especially his wife, for being in shock. They literally found out you existed this morning."

"I—" Mia was cut off before she could process what he had said.

"Also, due to David's massive amount of medical bills, treatments, and other legal expenses, unfortunately, there's no remaining estate to be divided among the family. The remaining part is a last farewell from David. He made a video before he died. We're ready now, so please come in."

He opened the door, and before Mia could respond, she felt his hand press into her back, helping to guide her into the room. He closed the door behind them. Mia stood still for a moment, examining the open area. Five people sat at a large mahogany conference table in the middle of the room. A few abstract paintings of distant buildings lined the walls, each framed in gold. Artificial potted plants were scattered around to give the room a more aesthetically pleasing feel. No one said anything to Mia after she entered, but all eyes were on her. There were no welcoming arms and not so much as a hug or a smile.

Mr. Lucas placed his hand on Mia's shoulder, signaling her to wait before being seated. He began introducing Mia to the individuals seated around the table. Toward the head of the table, two men sat together. Both were average-looking, casually dressed black men. Mr. Lucas introduced them as Nelson Ritter and Charles Suggs, David's two dearest friends and business partners. She smiled. They smiled and nodded back. At least two friendly people shared the room with her.

Mr. Lucas then pointed to the next person at the table. The woman looked visibly upset at the sight of Mia, apprehension and disgust plastered on her almond-shaped face. Tacky fashion jewelry covered her petite body, sparkling and reflecting off her dark, polished skin. The blonde synthetic wig on her head brushed across the padded shoulders of her black peplum blazer with every eye roll and head shake thrown in Mia's direction. Mr. Lucas cleared his throat at the sight of the woman's cold, unfriendly body language.

"This is David's *lovely* wife, Valerie Newell."

Mia said nothing. She looked away to the end of the table, where an elderly woman sat in a wheelchair next to a younger woman with deep russet skin, dressed in African printed scrubs. The old woman's head slumped on her chest, while appearing fast asleep. Her thick gray hair was pulled back, and she wore a long floral muumuu, her feet covered in pink bedroom slippers. Even though Mia could not fully see her face, she could tell by her wrinkled arms and hands she was well on in years. Liver spots and fading melanin covered her skin. Something about her intrigued Mia. Mr. Lucas announced, "This is our very own local celebrity journalist, Mrs. Sarah Newell, David's mother. Along with her nurse, Tracy."

Mia suddenly felt overwhelmed. *A grandmother? My grandmother? I do have a family!*

She once again felt Mr. Lucas' hand on her back, directing her to take a seat at the table. She quickly sat down in a chair across from Valerie, directing her attention to the plants around the room to avoid making awkward eye contact. Mr. Lucas remained by the door, pulling out some paperwork and a VHS videotape.

"Thank you all again for your attendance today. Now that we've cleared up certain legal matters with the business and finances, we will move on to a final farewell recorded by David."

Mr. Lucas slipped the tape into the VHS player on top of a large TV by the door. He pressed play, turned out one of the lights, and took his seat again.

At first, it was only an empty leather chair with a disorganized bookshelf in the background. Mia and the others waited for something to happen. Then a man, dressed in a dark blue suit, walked across the screen and sat down in the chair. Everyone in the room gasped, and Valerie began to weep. Mia covered her mouth, frozen in shock.

She'd never seen a picture of her father. Norma never gave her a detailed description of him before the night Mia confronted her. Mia had grown up knowing one fact about her father— that he was a black man. That vague and description-less piece of information was it. From then on, she viewed every stranger riding beside her in an elevator or sitting across from her on the train through the lens of possibility. Now her search was finally over. There he was. A stranger. Her father. She recognized herself in his deep brown eyes. He was the most handsome man she'd ever seen in her life. She now understood how Norma had fallen for him the way she did. Even though his eyes seemed to be sunken and dark, he still embodied everything her mother said he was the day she met him. David smiled, looking into the camera, sitting there as if to allow the room a moment to process his presence, knowing that he'd be gone when they saw him again at that moment.

Mr. Lucas paused the tape for Valerie to get her sobbing under control.

"Why, God? WHY! Why would you take my husband from me?" she screamed, banging her fist on the thick wooden table.

"Valerie, shut up!" a strong and heavy voice yelled from the other end of the table.

Mia flung her head around to find the old woman, Sarah, now very much alert. "All you've done since David died is whine and have a damn pity party! Why don't you shut the hell up and let someone else grieve for a change!"

Mia could tell at that moment that Sarah was not to be messed with, and everyone at the table knew it. Her voice rained down a rapture's fire, and Valerie was not in a place to escape the flames.

Valerie placed a tissue under her nose, nodded, and signaled for Mr. Lucas to continue the tape.

David started his speech by speaking to his business partners, Charles and Nelson. He thanked them for handling the business while he was in the hospital and for being there every day while he was sick. The two men stared with heavy hearts at the man they once knew but smiled that he was able to say goodbye to them one last time. David gave them instructions about how he'd like to see the successful bar they had started together continue. He pleaded with them never to give up, even after he was gone. The words of encouragement and love broke the two men down, and by the end of David's speech, they were crying and grieving for their friend.

David paused and hung his head for a moment. Up next was Valerie. He began with an apology that he had cheated on her all those years ago. It had been the hardest thing to keep from her, but he had made it his business to make it up to her every day, even though she never knew. He said that by the time he found out about Mia, the cancer was already spreading and that adding more pain to the situation would've been more than she could handle. He finished by telling her he loved her and that she was always his "little ray of sunshine." Valerie continued to weep into tissue after tissue.

David collected himself and began again with a message to his mother, Sarah. After yelling at Valerie, Sarah was wide awake. She watched the screen as her son expressed his thanks for her raising him and giving him the courage to become an entrepreneur. He continued by regaling the room with funny stories of his childhood with Sarah and how his mother's passion for writing and storytelling shaped his world. Mia looked back to see Sarah stone-faced. She could tell it wasn't from a lack of caring but a look of remorse that she'd lost her only child too soon. David's jokes and funny stories relieved some of the tension that had built up inside the room.

Finally, it was time for David to speak to Mia. His eyes stared into the camera as if he could see her through the lens. The anticipation clenched Mia's body. She wondered if the stranger would say anything to calm her restless nerves. She nudged her body to the edge of her chair in suspense.

"Hi Mia. By now, you should know who I am. I know this must be a lot for you, seeing me now, even though I'll be gone when you're watching this. Mia, I need you to know I never regretted meeting or being with your mother. She was a beautiful distraction and, dammit, if I didn't get pulled in. Valerie and I were having some issues in our marriage at the time. I had a weak moment. Shit, what can I say? I messed up, but I promise you I never knew you existed. I'm telling you, if I'd known, I would've been there for you every day while you were growing up.

"I don't fault Norma for not telling me. If you're mad at her, please don't be. I hurt her really bad. I hurt her more than any good woman should ever be hurt. I always wanted a kid, though. Val and I never had any luck, but here you are, already grown and beautiful. I've been sick for a few years and haven't traveled much, but when Norma told me about you, I knew I had to see you somehow. You never knew I was there, but I made it to your grad school graduation. Shit, I didn't even tell Norma I was coming. I was sick as a dog and had to have an IV bag in my arm the whole time, but I couldn't miss your big day. You looked so beautiful walking down to accept your degree. You looked just like your mother did the day I met her. I wanted so badly to hug you and tell you how proud I was of you, but I knew it would only cause you pain. So, I stayed dead to you, but just know I love you.

"I love you so much. You're the only kid I have. I will never stop watching over you and loving you. I've been calling Norma almost every day just to see how you're doing. I know she's getting sick of me calling. I got all your baby pictures and stuff your mom gave me right here.

"Dang man. Just thinking about all this blows my mind. This has been the hardest year of my life. Having to stay silent. Not being able to let you know, I thought about you every day. I wish I had more time. You still have your grandmother, though. Sarah is feisty, but give her some time to warm up to you. I know she will love you, too. I promise. I hope you are chasing your dreams and doing great things. You have greatness in you, Mia; I know you're going to do amazing things after I'm gone—no doubt about it.

"Oh, and I know Norma is probably not there with you. But Norma, if you are there, I apologize for hurting you. I know you had plans for law school, and I caused you to have to kill all of your dreams. I hope you and Mia don't hate me. I was young and dumb. If I could do it all over again, I would, just to get Mia in the end. I don't have much to leave you, unfortunately. All the money I would've been able to leave you belongs to these damn cancer treatment centers now. They aren't helping, and I can feel things going south. Thought I was going to make it to my 55th birthday, but I don't think that's going to happen. Mia, I didn't want you reading some piece of paper from me asking you to forgive me. I wanted you to see me. See my face and see my sincerity. I love you, Mia. I can't stress that to you enough. I hope one day you can forgive me. I'm asking for just an ounce of mercy, just an ounce of grace. I'm human, just like anyone else. Your forgiveness would mean everything to me. I'll rest easy knowing you'll forgive me one day."

The tape stopped, and the room fell into a deep silence.

CHAPTER SIX

REJECTED

Five minutes.

That was all she'd been given to see her father for the first time. Hear his voice for the first time. Process uncharted feelings for the first time. To go through anger, disappointment, and somehow forgiveness for the first time. Everything wrapped up in five overwhelming minutes.

Mr. Lucas began talking to the room, but Mia was far from paying attention.

"Well, that concludes everything on our agenda. Everyone will receive a copy of David's farewell in the mail within the next few weeks. I hope David's last words filled you with a sense of peace, knowing how much he cared for each of you. He will truly be missed."

With the final words delivered, Mr. Lucas turned off the TV and went to open the door for everyone to leave. Mia stood up, gathering her purse from the chair beside her. Charles walked over to Mia and reached out to shake her hand.

"It's a pleasure to meet David's daughter. He did nothing but talk about having kids for the longest time. I'm glad he found out you were alive before he died."

"Thank you very much, Mr. Suggs. I appreciate you telling me that." Mia smiled.

Nelson, too, reached out to shake Mia's hand and thanked her for coming. The two men walked over to Sarah, said their farewells, and left the room.

Mia watched as Sarah's nurse gathered their belongings and unlocked Sarah's wheelchair to leave. Sarah seemed to have fallen back asleep. Mia did not want to disturb her after the outburst earlier and turned her attention to Valerie in the corner, getting her coat and purse from the coat rack. She walked slowly over to Valerie, naively hoping that she'd be a little more compassionate now after everyone had heard David's message. The sight of Mia coming towards her resurrected the apprehensive look on her face. She put her hand up, signaling Mia to stop.

"Listen, Mya."

"It's *Mia*." She folded her arms, growing tired of Valerie's rudeness towards her.

"Whatever. Listen, I know you probably want to chit-chat and all that crap, but you'll have to excuse me for not wanting to talk. I just found out this morning that the man I have dedicated my entire life to cheated on me. Not just cheated but had a kid! The one thing I couldn't give him. There's nothing you or anyone else can say to make me feel better. I don't want to talk to you or anyone else right now. Just leave me alone!"

Valerie began crying again and brushed past Mia, her heels tapping wildly as she rushed out of the building. Mia was left standing alone, unsure of how to feel. She decided to forgo speaking to anyone else there, fearing they would reject her. She hung her head and turned to walk out the door.

"She's a piece of work, isn't she?" A voice behind Mia chuckled. She turned back to see Sarah awake again, smiling at her. Sarah's deep brown eyes restored the sense of peace Mia needed. They reminded her of her father's eyes, a place where she could find solace. She walked over to sit down next to Sarah, hoping for more of her light to brighten the darkness Valerie had left behind.

"She always has to make every damn thing about her. Oh Lord, I can't have a baby! Oh Lord, my husband cheated on me! Hell, I'm surprised David didn't do it sooner and more often! Dealing with that crazy fool every day. I couldn't wait for her to shut the hell up!"

"She hates me," said Mia.

"She doesn't hate you, child. She's just jealous right now. Jealous that she tried a lifetime to do what your momma got done in one night. She's jealous and green with envy. To top it off, she probably came here thinking David had some money left to give her. She sure struck out today! Lord, you have a sense of humor!" Sarah laughed so hard she abruptly started coughing.

"Take it easy, Sarah," Tracy urged.

"Oh, hush, Tracy, I'm fine. I'm fine!" Tracy handed Sarah a napkin to wipe her mouth.

"It's wonderful to meet you, Sarah. I've never met any of my other family members. It's great to meet my grandmother. My actual grandmother!" Mia became giddy and excited, repeating the word *grandmother* over and over in her head.

"Ain't that much about me that's *grand*, child. I'm not the woman I used to be, that's for sure. I'm just an old lump of skin, sitting in a wheelchair."

Mia could see Sarah's eyes getting heavy. Her head slumped back onto her chest. Mia tried to blurt out what she wanted to say.

"I know you have to leave, but do you think I could come to see you sometime? I would love to get to know you better and just, you know, talk."

"That… that's…" Sarah's words slurred as she dozed back off to sleep. Tracy leaned over, placing her hand on Mia's shoulder.

"It's her medication, Mia," said Tracy. "I need to get her back home so she can rest. Today has been a long day for us both."

"I understand. May I come see her tomorrow before I head back to New York?"

"Sarah doesn't normally allow visitors. Her own personal wishes. The only person she ever allowed to come see her was David. She has made it painfully clear not to let anyone else in, not even extended family. I'm going to have to say no for now."

Mia grabbed a piece of paper from the table and jotted down her phone number for Tracy. "Please, can you call me if she ever changes her mind?"

Tracy nodded in agreement and pushed the paper into the pocket of her scrubs. Mia stepped aside to allow Tracy and Sarah to exit the room. Mia followed a few steps behind, hoping Sarah would wake up before they left the building, but she remained asleep even as Tracy loaded her into the van in the parking lot and drove away.

The stir of people leaving the office had settled. Aside from Phyllis, who was busy tending to her work in the back office, Mia was now alone. The journey she had once been so elated to take was over, and the thought of returning home empty-handed crushed her once hopeful spirit. Coming to Virginia was supposed to yield something more than what she'd been given. Something or someone to start fresh with. Something that would send her back to New York more fulfilled than before she left.

As overwhelming as the moment was, there was one thing she gained that would never leave her memory. David. She remembered her father's eyes and the sense of calm that revived her, a calm that subdued her fears and eased her anxiety. If David were her only reward from her journey, she would accept that. She collected her thoughts and belongings and headed out to find a hotel room for the night.

As Mia shuffled towards the exit, she heard Phyllis calling from the back room.

"Wait, Mia! I was just about to lock up. How did everything go in there?"

"I guess it went okay. My father left a message for me to watch. I'm not sure how to really process it all right now. I'm heading to find a hotel for the night. Then I'll head home in the morning."

"There are some great hotels downtown. I can give you the name of one I normally send clients to." Phyllis placed a folder under her arm, reached into her bag, pulled out a pen and a piece of paper, and began jotting down the address. "Are you going to go see your grandmother again before you leave?"

"I would love to, but Tracy told me she doesn't like to have visitors. No matter who they are."

Phyllis paused her writing and smiled, looking up at Mia. "Oh, really?" She chuckled. "Well, just so happens I might have a golden ticket for you. Here," Phyllis grabbed the manila folder and handed it to Mia. "Your grandmother forgot the paperwork she signed earlier. I was going to stop by the post office on my way home and have them mailed to her, but you could use this as your opportunity to see her!"

"Are you sure that will be okay?"

"I don't see why not! All you need to do is drop them off. I have her address here on the front of the folder. It's about an hour away. When you get there, you can try to see if she's willing to change her mind about seeing you. It's up to you, but this is the best option without you technically going against her wishes."

Phyllis placed her hand on Mia's shoulder, giving her a look of reassurance. Mia reluctantly agreed, and the two women went their separate ways. She wasn't thrilled to hear the location was an hour from Richmond. She wanted to go home to begin the daunting task of drafting an exhibit proposal for the museum's grand opening and to stay employed. However, she had the ticket she needed to see Sarah again, and she didn't want to waste it. To talk to her and not return home feeling so empty-handed. Mia latched onto hope. *Tracy has got to let me see her now!*

CHAPTER SEVEN

SARAH

Mia had gotten little sleep that night. Emotions sat heavily on her chest, and she spent the hours of moonlit darkness staring at the decorative square ceiling tiles of her hotel room.

She had taken Phyllis' advice and stayed at a nice but overpriced hotel downtown. The sounds of cars honking and people shouting from the streets below reminded Mia of home. She wasn't sure what she was feeling. If asked to describe it, she'd choose to remain silent, afraid of letting awkward words dilute what she felt. There were no accurate words she could use for any of it. She knew she wanted nothing more than to see Sarah again, but something about Sarah gave her a gnawing feeling. She kept trying to solve the mystery of why Sarah refused to see anyone other than David. Why did she want to shut the world out? Did Sarah want to shut her out, too? This went on for hours until she found a space in her overthinking to fall asleep.

The sun's light soon crept in to greet Mia, and she instantly regretted her restless night. Although she was groggy and exhausted, she did her best to get dressed, pack, and get out the door to make the hour-long drive. Mia looked again at the address on the folder. The facility was in Charlottesville. She'd never been to Charlottesville but was determined to get to Sarah. Before leaving the building, she stopped at the hotel's front desk to ask for printed directions. A plump and cheerful woman behind the desk greeted Mia with a smile and happily printed out the directions for her. Mia slipped into the breakfast area and grabbed a cup of coffee and a Danish.

After an hour of stop-and-go traffic, unintentional detours, and hot coffee spills, she reached her destination. A large sign in front of a gravel road read,

Lakeside Nursing Home: Your home away from home!

Mia inched down the gravel entrance way. Her head moved left and right, observing the buildings and residents scattered across the grounds. She was momentarily overtaken by the beauty of all that was laid out before her. The trees and bushes were aligned and trimmed with care. The leaves glowed in the sunlight with beautiful shades of yellow, orange, and red. There were rows and rows of pansies and petunias that gave vibrant life to the withering world around them. The grass was full and weedless. Mia couldn't spot a single flaw. As she pulled into the parking lot, she looked ahead to the main building, aged with time and full of nostalgia for the Old Antebellum South. The Greek Revival-style building was a massive edifice. Wrapped in beautifully aligned white columns, riddled with windows on every side, with a long, peaceful porch that offered shade from the sun.

Mia nervously parked the car and stepped out, taking in deep breaths of the fresh, vintage air. She rarely, if ever, got the opportunity to enjoy scenes like this. The air was clean and crisp, unlike the air in the city. She admired it all, piece by piece, momentarily forgetting where she was and why she was there. Her trance was broken by a firm tap on her shoulder. She turned around to find Tracy standing behind her. Mia smiled, admiring Tracy's vibrant earrings, African-print scrubs, and natural, picked-out afro.

"Hello, Mia. What brings you here?" Tracy's rigid tone was far from welcoming. Mia could tell by watching Tracy load Sarah into the van the previous day she was a small but strong woman, easily capable of physically throwing Mia off the property. Despite Mia's hope that she would be welcomed with open arms, the concerned look on Tracy's face proved otherwise.

"Hi, Tracy. Umm…Sarah forgot some paperwork yesterday, and Phyllis asked if I could bring it by for her."

"Mia, I thought I told you yesterday that Sarah has requested not to have any visitors. We have to respect our residents' wishes."

Mia paused, trying to think of a way around the hurdle placed in front of her.

"I drove all the way from New York, Tracy," Mia pleaded. "Could you ask her if I can see her? I won't stay long, I promise."

Tracy sighed, rolling her eyes. "If she starts up and has any outbursts or problems, you'll have to leave, Mia."

Mia nodded in agreement. The two women walked into the building side by side. Mia looked around the lobby, which was just as elegant and detailed as the building's exterior. A stunning entryway, lined with gold chandeliers, welcomed her. Large, elegant tapestries hung along each wall, depicting scenes of lush gardens and quaint countryside kitchens. The wooden floor shone and sparkled, proud of its fresh coat of wax. It was evident that Lakeside Nursing Home was where wealthy people came to live out their final years.

Tracy signaled Mia to take a seat in the lobby waiting area while she went to Sarah's room to speak with her. Mia grasped the folder to her chest and waited patiently for Tracy to return. She watched residents come and go from the building and eavesdropped on nearby conversations from other nurses and staff. *Mrs. Jenkins needs a new bedpan. Mr. Knowles needs his medication. Mrs. Andrews doesn't like bread pudding.* Mia smiled at the passersby, patiently waiting for Tracy to return.

She worried that Tracy had forgotten about her as she looked at her phone, realizing that thirty minutes had passed. Mia stood up, planning to go find Tracy herself, but stopped after spotting her coming down the hall. Mia was relieved to see a smile forming in the corner of Tracy's mouth.

"She's having an okay day today. She said she'd be okay with seeing you." Tracy placed her hand on Mia's shoulder, leading her down the hallway to Sarah's room.

Each step Mia took felt heavier than the last as the two women walked down a dimly lit, narrow hallway. Smaller, elegant tapestries lined the deep-blue painted walls. The wooden floorboards creaked and moaned under the weight of their feet.

"This building is over 150 years old," Tracy noted, looking back at Mia. "These old oak floors are from the original building. The owners kept them even after two major renovations. They do some horrible creaking, but they are still going strong."

"Yeah, they sound really old," Mia whispered.

They stopped at a closed door with *Room 129* printed on the front. Tracy opened the door to reveal the room. Mia stood in the doorway, admiring the space's contents. Her senses became overwhelmed by a rush of various sights and smells that instantly greeted her. The walls were covered with random trinkets and knick-knacks, tightly packed on thick wooden floating shelves. An array of abstract paintings of different shapes and sizes hung between the shelves. The artist had splashed random bursts of acrylic color across a few canvases. Mia then turned her attention to the hardwood floor, covered with an oversized hand-knotted Oriental rug. Deep black wheelchair marks made unpleasant tracks across the once vibrant crimson-red wool fabric. Pressed up against the wall was a large couch with plush seats, its fabric worn by time. There were small wooden end tables placed between the couch and a set of velvet-upholstered accent chairs. Two beautifully decorated crazed ceramic vases stood tall in separate corners of the room. Mia instantly fell in love with the art and eclectic items scattered around the room. There was a strong mint scent in the air, and Mia noticed several potted mint plants on the windowsills. Everything seemed out of place and yet somehow in order. Lost in another moment of discovery, Mia felt Tracy tap her on the shoulder, signaling her to walk into the room.

"Sarah," Tracy called out. "Mia's here to see you. Where did you go?"

A voice from behind another door in the room called out to Tracy, "I'm here, woman! Give an old lady a moment to get there!"

Tracy walked to the bedroom door and opened it, allowing Sarah to wheel herself out. Mia instantly felt butterflies dance in her stomach. She anxiously watched Sarah struggle to wheel herself out of the bedroom, a noticeable irritation on her face. Sarah's gray hair had been pinned up at the lawyer's office, but now it lay thick and untamed on her shoulders. Her nightgown and slippers were a matching shade of weathered pink.

Tracy reached out to offer her help, but Sarah swatted her away.

"I can do it, dammit! Leave me be!"

"As you wish," Tracy muttered.

Sarah came to a stop in the middle of the room, looking Mia up and down. Mia remained quiet, allowing Sarah to examine her like a piece of artwork on display.

"You look like David. You must be David's. I didn't believe it, but dammit, if you don't have those eyes."

"Yes, ma'am," Mia responded. "I appreciate you allowing me to come and see you."

"Well, I've been here, wasting away. Not much to see. Tracy said you have some papers for me." Sarah reached out a visibly shaking hand to Mia.

Mia handed the folder to Sarah, who then brandished it before Tracy.

"Read that stuff, Tracy. I don't want to make you feel left out." The annoyed look on Tracy's face made Mia look away. She opened the folder and read through its contents.

"Looks like it's the paperwork and receipts about David's funeral you signed when we were there. They're marked that everything has been finalized."

"Good, good," Sarah said. "Dealing with that damn Valerie has been hell. I know it sounds horrible, but I'm glad it's all over. That's all you wanted, child?"

Mia stood frozen, scared to speak. She was afraid to ask Sarah's permission to stay. She wanted to stay in the cluttered room and be next to Sarah for as long as she could, but finding the courage to ask was something she couldn't bring herself to do.

"I...umm..." she muttered timidly.

"Spit it out! I don't have all day!"

"I...I would like to stay a little longer and talk, if that's okay?" Sarah rolled her eyes and looked up at Tracy.

"She drove all the way from New York, Sarah. Give her a few moments. Don't be mean."

"I'm not mean. I'm old!" Sarah rolled herself over to a table in the kitchen area.

"Well, have a seat, girl and don't touch anything."

Tracy smiled, whispering sarcastically to Mia, "Have fun!" and walked out of the room, closing the door behind her.

CHAPTER EIGHT

INSECURE

Silence.

A silence that felt uneasy, stirring anxiety. Like the quiet after a flash of lightning, waiting for the thunder to crash.

Mia watched Sarah from across the table, nervously waiting for the thunder to shake the room. Sarah had taken her attention away from Mia and fixed her sights on an orange in a stained-glass fruit bowl on the table. Her shaking hands botched every attempt to peel the orange. She fumbled it around, muttering curse words under her breath, making no attempt to ask for help. Mia felt sorry for her. She could tell Sarah was one of those people who would reject any help, just to prove a point. She was stubborn. Set in her ways and didn't care who knew it. Several minutes passed, and Mia decided she'd seen enough. She extended her hand, silently asking Sarah to hand over the piece of fruit. Sarah huffed but complied, rolling the orange across to Mia.

"I could've done it," she huffed. "This damn medicine makes it hard to do things, that's all. Makes me shake and move slow. I hate it!"

"It's okay, I don't mind," Mia said softly, trying to calm Sarah.

"Well, I do mind," Sarah folded her arms as she waited impatiently for Mia to finish.

"What do you want? I told Tracy I don't like people in my room. Looking at me like I'm crazy or something. Looking at my things like I'm some kind of old bag lady. These things mean a lot to me. They belong to me."

Mia finished peeling the orange, divided it, and handed it back to Sarah.

"I came to spend some time with you. Maybe get to know you a little better. I don't have any other family. Just you and my mother."

Sarah rolled her eyes. "David said your momma never knew he was married. Is that right?"

"Yes, ma'am. That's what my mom said, too."

"Well, I guess I can't talk too much shit about her then. David had his ways, at least before he married Valerie. I never believed him to be faithful to her all those years. He loved the ladies too much. Always was the ladies' man. Always had his eye on the next one, even if one was standing beside him. Then came Valerie, and God only knows why he fell for her the way he did."

Mia began recalling the story her mother had told her about David. She surprised herself by going to bat for Norma, presenting a case that Norma had once been a good person, not the tramp her grandmother had probably made her out to be. Sarah sat quietly, eating her orange and fading in and out of interest. It was a scarce moment of clarity for her, one free of the fogginess of medications and age. Although well on in years, Sarah was sharp and had a keen sense of discernment. Even though she sensed Mia wasn't a threat, she couldn't bring herself to let Mia in at that moment. Life had chiseled away at her once cheerful exterior. Bad days had become more frequent than good days. Her callous temperament was now permanent. Family or not, Sarah was going to make it her business to push Mia away. There was no space in her heart for anyone else but David, and now that he was gone, she was ready to shut everyone out completely. She examined Mia from head to toe, looking for something to criticize. Anything to hurt her enough so she would leave and never come back, giving Sarah the chance to retreat into her safe haven of solitude.

Her eyes soon landed on Mia's hair. Mia's *fake* hair. Her irritation grew, the wig fueling her irrational fury. The thought of Mia not appreciating her natural beauty disgusted Sarah. She threw her hand up, commanding Mia to stop talking.

"If you are going to sit here with me, you'd better take that ridiculous-looking mop off your head! I won't have insecure people in my presence!" Sarah pointed to Mia's wig.

"My wig?" asked Mia, confused.

"Yes, the wig! Why are you wearing someone else's hair when you have your own? You don't appreciate what God gave you?"

"I…I guess. I mean, I don't really like my real hair. It's difficult to deal with." Mia's voice cracked with embarrassment. She moved her hand around her head, patting the wig to ensure it was in place.

"Well, that bird's nest doesn't have a place at this table. Take it off or get out!"

Sarah leaned back in her chair, feeling accomplished, assured that her callous threat had worked. Like a wolf seeing fear in its prey, she folded her arms and prepared to watch Mia submit, but Sarah couldn't have been more wrong. She didn't know Mia or the lengths Mia had gone through to sit at that table with her. To her amazement, she watched as Mia began removing the bobby pins and pulled off the wig. She unraveled the few fuzzy cornrows that lined her head and ran her fingers through the tangled strands.

In that moment, Sarah knew Mia was unsinkable. Maybe her discernment was right. Mia wasn't a threat, and maybe someone she could allow in. After all, she was David's daughter. Sarah sighed and thought to herself about what letting Mia in meant for her. Her past was riddled with pain, loss, and a secret she'd held onto for decades. She had never told another living soul. Not even David. Sarah was not ready to shed the weight she carried. Nor was she sure if Mia was someone she could trust. But if Mia could show bravery, she too could let her guard down for a moment and be kind. Sarah unfolded her arms, leaning forward to look into Mia's deep brown eyes.

"That's much better. I can see you now."

CHAPTER NINE

REVEALED

Mia had been exposed. Although feeling uneasy, there was nowhere else she'd rather be than exposed in front of Sarah. She couldn't remember the last time she had let anyone other than Bee see her without her wig. She could feel the cool, minty air finding its way onto her scalp. It felt good.

"May we continue?" Mia asked, pushing the wig to the edge of the table.

Sarah nodded.

Mia thought for a few moments about what to ask. She had dozens of questions for Sarah, but wanted to make the most out of the time they had together, so she would tread lightly.

"Mr. Lucas said something about you being a local celebrity. How did that happen?"

Sarah rolled her eyes and reached over to one of the potted plants, pulling a stem of mint leaves from the dirt. She brushed off the crinkly green leaves and placed the fragrant stem in her mouth to chew on.

"Everyone makes such a fuss about it. I'm not famous; they just love to make old people feel like we still matter. I moved to Richmond with my late husband decades ago. I got a job writing for a local newspaper after we settled in. It was meant to be a way to pass the time, but it became much more. They sure didn't love me back when I started writing about Civil Rights. Getting stories from people who were being beaten and harassed, all because they wanted to be treated fairly. I was a problem to them then. I got death threats and evil looks everywhere I went. But as I got older, and the world started to change, people around here started to change their minds about me. I got some awards for my work—some pats on the back. The city even dubbed me a *local treasure* for all the work I did. I exposed lies and brought the truth to light. I guess they wanted to feel better about the hell they neglected to mention they put me through. The mayor gave me permanent residence here in this uppity-ass nursing home. I just smiled and took it. I wanted to spit on them, but beggars can't be choosy. It's a hell of a lot better than that dump Valerie wanted to put me in. So, here I am."

"Sounds like you have been through a lot."

"I wrote to make sure that people knew the truth, that's all."

"May I call you Grandma?" Mia blurted out.

"No. You make me sound like some old woman," Sarah scoffed.

"Okay, no problem. I'll stick to—"

"I guess you can call me…Sadie. That's what your father used to call me." Sarah sucked her teeth as the unpleasant taste of vulnerability filled her mouth.

"Okay, Sadie. I have so much I want to talk to you about. I don't know where to start."

"I don't like to talk much anymore, but ask what you need to, child. I'll try to answer what I can."

"Well, can you tell me more about my dad? What was he like when he was young? Do you have any pictures of him? Was he smart? Did he go to college?"

"Slow down, child, slow down! I'll tell you what you want to know. Better yet..." Sarah paused, looking at a small closet by the doorway. "Go into that closet, and get me that big tote box on the floor, and don't touch anything else!" Mia did as she was told and retrieved a hefty tote. Its contents were too much for Mia to pick up, so she dragged it, step by step, back to the table beside Sarah.

"I want you to know I haven't opened this box in years. I stopped taking pictures of David or anyone else a long time ago. I want to remember him the way he was before he got those sunken eyes. You can go on and dig in there for the ones I have of him."

Sarah ran her hand along the top of the box, remembering David and the day he helped her slide it and all her memories into the closet to be locked away for good. She was sure the pictures and other aged mementos would break her down, but she refused to let Mia see her cry. She lifted her hand, instructing Mia to remove the lid.

The smell of old books and the earthy, oaky scent of the contents immediately hit them. Mia was taken aback by the vast number of old pictures, letters and a few journals that lay within. She slowly pulled photos out of the box, one by one, placing them on the table. Sarah watched as Mia laid out memories from her life. There were photographs of old friends and other people she once knew. Moments in time that had meant something to her. She cared not to look at them. To her, they no longer served a purpose. The once-cherished faces that smiled at her in the photos were now strangers' faces. She was only interested in the pictures of David. She slid the unwanted photos to the left and right of her until she came to a picture of herself holding David in her arms. She flipped the photograph over to reveal its inscription: *Home from the hospital, David b. 1949.*

"Here," she said to Mia. "This is David and me a few days after he was born." She passed the fading photo to Mia, who scooped it up with delight.

"I have more in there. Got some of David and his daddy. My husband passed away when David was young. Got some of David in school too." Sarah knew Mia would not let up until she bled every memory dry.

She told Mia about the day David was born and what it was like being a mother for the first time. No matter the circumstances, Sarah did her best to raise her only child after her husband's sudden passing. She told Mia about the fun times and how much she enjoyed being a mother. She spoke of the hard times when money was scarce, but she and David had made it through. Her memories of David were still fresh. Mia soaked up all the stories that Sarah shared, not minding anything else but her grandmother's voice. Every word from Sarah's mouth filled Mia's heart with joy. As Sarah continued, Mia felt increasingly connected to her grandmother and her father. She felt good that her father didn't have to grow up in a cold and loveless home like she had. He was loved, and Mia loved Sarah even more for that.

Sarah poured out her words as she touched each picture, explaining the background and story of each scene. Her words painted vivid images, bringing every scene to life right there in the room. Mia noticed how Sarah spoke with such flair and poise as she told her stories. Only a short time ago, her speech had been full of curse words and rude outbursts. Without thinking, Mia blurted out exactly what she was thinking to Sarah, interrupting her train of thought.

"Sadie, you speak so well! You make me feel like I'm listening to a narrated story!"

"Just because I'm old doesn't mean I'm dumb!"

"I'm… I'm sorry," Mia's voice broke again with embarrassment. "I didn't mean it that way; I just—"

Sarah put her hand up again, signaling Mia to be quiet.

"I know what you meant, child. One minute, I'm cursing up a storm, and in the next minute, I'm as smooth as Zora Neale Hurston. I learned a long time ago from someone very dear to my heart that every word in a story deserves detail. People have to feel the words, not just hear them. It's one reason I became a writer. I love giving life to words. While working for the newspapers, it was my job to create scenes that people could feel while they were reading my stories. I speak the way I see things. Those polished words help those who aren't able to see what I see. My words outside of my stories are mine. They belong to me. Nothing wrong with sprinkling a few curse words here and there. It's good for the soul. I may be old, but not old enough that I have lost my touch!"

"I understand," replied Mia. "I'm not judging you; I just don't curse much. My mom always did enough of that for both of us."

"Well, hell, maybe you should try it sometime!"

Mia shook her head and continued digging through the box for more pictures. A knock at the door interrupted them. Mia stepped away from the table to see who was there.

"You stay put, child," Sarah said, tapping the table. "I can get it myself. My arms need a little exercise anyway. Go on and look at whatever you want in there."

Sarah used what strength she had to turn her wheelchair away from the table and towards the door. She opened it to find a nurse greeting her with news that lunch was now ready and being served. Sarah didn't seem particularly excited. She began interrogating the young orderly about the menu and about how she had been severely disappointed with yesterday's entrée choices.

Mia paid no attention to the two at the door and continued shuffling through the photos and letters in the tote. She reached down, this time hitting something hard with her hand. She brushed the items aside to find a shoebox wrapped in several pieces of red twine. Mia realized that the person who had tied the string had entangled the box so thoroughly that no one else could open it. Mia pulled the box from the rest of the contents and set it on the table. She looked it over, each side without any visible markings or words to explain why it was sealed. The contents of the shoebox were light, as Mia shook it to try to guess what was hidden inside. She looked over to the door, seeing that Sarah and the nurse were still at odds about whether Sarah should leave her room to eat. Mia's curiosity gripped her. She remembered Sarah saying she could look at *anything* in the tote, so she must've meant that, too. Something in her was pushing her hands closer to a pair of scissors by the fruit bowl on the table. She quickly slipped her fingers into the two cold holes of the metal scissors and began cutting into the tangled twine. Pieces fell to the floor. Mia lifted the lid of the box, exposing its contents, and gasped!

CHAPTER TEN

ASHAMED

Of all the items inside the weathered shoebox, it was a tattered photograph of a deceased man in a casket that took Mia by surprise. The stranger lay peacefully, dressed in a blue suit and tie. Death terrified Mia. Her startled gasp caught Sarah's attention. She shooed the nurse away and rolled herself back to the table. Sarah lowered her eyes to see the red twine scattered on the table and floor. The culprit sat still in her chair, covering her mouth, unable to plead her case. Sarah looked at her with disappointment.

"This is the thanks I get, huh? For you to go behind my back and open something that was clearly meant to be kept closed? If you wanted to know what was in the box so badly, why not just ask me?" Sarah was calm, too calm. Her stillness frightened Mia more than if she'd yelled at her. She felt terrible and ashamed as she parted her mouth with trembling words.

"I...I...I thought you would be okay with me opening it. You said I could look at anything in the box. I'm so sorry. I don't know what I was thinking. I know you're upset. I'll go now."

Mia grabbed her belongings and fumbled awkwardly towards the door, almost knocking over one of the vases. She was too ashamed to be there any longer. She reached for the door handle but stopped when she heard Sarah speak again.

"That man. That dead man. That's my uncle, Martin. My mother's baby brother. He died in the war. Got his legs shot off. That's the only picture she had of him. Why would I want to see him like that? Why would I want to see any of the people I once loved like that?" Sarah wiped her eyes.

"That shoebox belonged to my mother before she passed away. I wrapped it up because I want no part of what's in there—pictures of people I remember, now dead and gone. I want it to stay closed."

Sarah wheeled herself closer to the kitchen table. She pressed her shaking hands into the scattered photos on the table and pushed them close to the edge. "Put everything back in the tote and close that shoebox, child. We're done."

Mia walked back to the table to clean up the mess she'd made. She tried not to make any eye contact with Sarah. Mia collected each photo, trying to etch each scene in her mind to recall later. Just when the lid of the tote was almost in place, another photo stuck to the top came loose and fell to the floor. Mia reached down to pick it up. She flipped it around to see a picture of two young women smiling and holding hands. An inscription on the back of the photo read, *Sarah and Claudette. Virginia Negro Studies Project, 1937.*

"Is this you, Sadie?" Mia asked. "You look so happy! Who's this woman with you?" Sarah snatched the photo from Mia and put it and the lid back in place.

"I said we're done now," Sarah snapped. "I don't want to talk about these things. I don't want to talk anymore; you got that?" Mia shook her head. An awkward silence filled the room.

Sarah could feel herself floating into uncharted waters with Mia. She'd always been strong and fearless, never letting her guard down for anyone. Why was this girl, this stranger, causing her to feel anything different? She hated to admit how much of herself she saw in Mia. She could hear a familiar voice, reminding her of who she once was and of the peace Mia could offer. She wanted to trust Mia. She wanted to be free of the weight she carried. To tell someone the truth once and for all. Sarah rolled herself to the doorway, leaving Mia behind at the table. She propped open the door and snapped her fingers.

"Well, don't just stand there looking stupid; it's lunchtime, child. Take me to the cafeteria!"

CHAPTER ELEVEN

SECRETS

Inside the open, airy cafeteria, warm sunlight trickled through the glass atrium ceiling. Rows of tables and stands, laden with a variety of food options, filled the space. The walls were painted the same shade of deep blue and garnished with faux autumn leaves and lifeless green vines. Residents were scattered in every direction. Some ate their easily digestible lunches alone, content with the solitude. Some were socializing and discussing the day's activities. Others rested peacefully at their tables with their heads nestled on their chests.

Mia pushed Sarah to an open table, asking her what she'd like to eat for lunch. Sarah was still sour toward Mia, but she gave her a detailed list of what she wanted and what she didn't. Mia did her best to mentally jot down Sarah's requests, making clear notations of the "don'ts". The last thing she wanted to do was upset Sarah more than she already was. Mia began making her way about the cafeteria, gathering items for her and Sarah to eat. While collecting some oranges from a fruit table, she spotted Tracy across from her.

"Oh, hi, Mia," Tracy said, waving. "What happened to your hair?"

"She made me take my wig off. She said I can't wear it around her." Tracy chuckled and walked around the table, putting her hand on Mia's shoulder to comfort her.

"That doesn't surprise me. She can get upset about the most trivial things. Well, other than that, how are things going between you two?"

"Well…I got her to speak to me. We looked at old photos and talked about my dad and other things. It was great, but I think I got on her bad side again. I don't think she's thrilled with my being here anymore. I'm just waiting for her to kick me out now, I guess."

"She isn't all that bad. She has her good days and bad days. Don't pay her any mind. I sure don't."

"I know, I know. I just…I want to know everything about her. She had no problem telling me about my dad and everything she remembered from his childhood. Now, when I ask her about her life, you know, before my dad, she shuts down. I got a few things out of her, but not much. Do you have any suggestions?"

"Well, has she told you about her slave stories yet?"

"Slave stories? What do you mean by *slave stories*?" Tracy leaned in closer to Mia to keep the conversation private.

"She doesn't talk about it to everyone, but when she first got here, she tried to tell a few other nurses and me about a slave woman she'd met when she was younger. Something about a project in Hampton, slaves, and a bunch of other stuff, but no one paid her any attention. Sarah was on a different medication then and was all types of loopy. I'm sure it was her imagination running wild. After we got her medication corrected, she stopped talking about it. I asked her if she still wanted to talk about it, but she refused, saying she knew we thought she was crazy and that she was lying. I didn't think she had been lying. Maybe she'd been recalling scenes from a book she'd read a long time ago. Or even exaggerating a story she wrote for a newspaper article. She seemed pretty passionate about it, so maybe you can start there and see if she opens up about more stuff. She's a feisty one, though. Don't let that wheelchair fool you! Almost ninety years old and has the mind of a steel trap! Nothing gets past her. Good luck to you if you can get her to open up."

"I'll make sure to ask her about it when the time is right," Mia whispered back to Tracy. "How long can I stay with her?"

"Normally, you'd have to leave after visiting hours are over. My boss doesn't play around with that rule, but you're in luck. She's out of town this week on vacation." Tracy patted Mia on the back in thanks. "Since you're so graciously keeping Sarah out of my hair, you can stay. As long as Sarah's okay with you staying in her room, I don't mind. We only have about three other nurses who work this wing of the building, so I will make sure they know about you. Just be sure to keep a low profile and don't make me regret my decision. I'll be in later to make sure she takes her medication."

Mia thanked Tracy as she headed off to tend to the other residents.

Mia grabbed the rest of the food for herself and Sarah and headed back to the table. She set everything before Sarah and sat down.

"It's about time. You took all day!" huffed Sarah.

"I saw Tracy at the table. We chatted for a few moments. She said…" Mia paused, momentarily deciding that maybe it was not the best time to bring up the conversation that she and Tracy had. She quickly changed the subject. "She said to tell you hi."

Sarah picked her way through the items Mia collected for her—a few pastries, some oranges, and sugar-free apple juice. Mia grabbed a ham sandwich and some tomato soup, content with finding something that wasn't mashed up or sugar-free. The two women sat silently across from one another, hoping someone would make the first move to speak. It was Sarah who finally tired of the silence.

"So, you've been in my business all day, picking through my pictures, but you've yet to tell me much of anything about you. Makes me wonder about you."

"What would you like to know?"

"Start from the beginning...that should give me time to eat this food."

Mia was eager to open up to Sarah, hoping she would act as a compassionate therapist. The session began with her sharing her life as a museum curator in New York, mentioning her best friend, Bee, and reminiscing about college and graduating with honors. She then discussed Norma, revealing her difficult childhood and the selfish lie she had carried her entire life, which took up much of the conversation. Talking about her mother remained a sensitive subject. Although first hesitant to discuss her condition, she eventually revealed her struggles with anxiety attacks but expressed gratitude, noting that since meeting Sarah, she'd been free of the attacks.

Sarah laughed at Mia attributing anything positive to her. "I don't want you giving me credit where it's not due. I don't turn water into wine, and I don't heal the blind!"

Mia laughed as Sarah jokingly waved her hand over her water glass, easing some of the tension that had built up between them. Mia realized that she'd been talking for so long that the cafeteria was almost empty.

"Are you finished?" Mia asked. "I can clean this up and take you back to the room if you want."

"That would be nice. I'm getting tired. I need to take a nap."

Mia cleaned up the mess that Sarah had made in front of her. Crumbs and orange peels lay everywhere. Mia was careful not to drop anything into Sarah's lap.

They returned to Sarah's room, both full and ready to rest.

"I can stay here and sleep on the couch while you take your nap. Would that be okay?"

"Whatever. Just don't bother me while I'm sleeping." Sarah yawned. "Push me to my bed; my arms are getting tired." Mia complied, pushing Sarah into the small bedroom and helping her onto her twin-sized bed. Mia reached for a lamp on the nightstand. The room was dark and windowless. Sarah reached over, smacking the back of Mia's hand.

"Keep that light off, hear! You can see just fine with the light from the living room. I don't want you turning on my lights in here. I like the dark, got that?"

Mia said nothing. She rubbed the back of her hand, feeling the heated sting of Sarah's slap.

"And don't get any bright ideas snooping through those pictures while I'm asleep. I'll know if you did!" Sarah growled.

"Yes, ma'am. I won't."

Mia looked at Sarah, lying down, vulnerable, unable to fight back at that moment. She decided to ask Sarah about the stories Tracy had mentioned. Sitting on the edge of the bed, she clasped her hands together as if praying for courage.

"Maybe when you get up, you can tell me about some of your other stories. Like the ones you told Tracy and the other nurses."

"What stories? What are you talking about, child?"

"The slave stories," Mia replied. Sarah propped herself up on the soft linens, staring at Mia in disbelief.

"Who…who told you about that?" Mia became unsettled at the change in Sarah's voice.

"Um…Tracy. Tracy told me you had other stories to tell. I would love to hear about them."

Sarah continued to stare into Mia's naïve eyes. Mia could see the tears beginning to form in the corners of her wrinkled eyelids. Sarah hung her head and rolled over, her back now facing Mia.

"You don't know when to shut up, do you? Just go. Shut the door behind you. I'm tired."

Mia rose from the side of the bed and left the room, closing the door behind her. She once again felt as though she had ruined everything and just wanted to find some way to stop those awkward moments from happening. She grabbed a large throw blanket from the side of the couch, pressed her face into the cushions, and cried herself to sleep.

CHAPTER TWELVE

VULNERABLE

Mia awoke to a knock at the door.

She sat up, squinting her eyes to adjust to the setting sunlight beaming from the window. Rubbing life back into her tear-stained face, she looked at a small analog clock perched on one of the floating shelves. She was surprised by how quickly almost two hours had passed. She hopped up from the couch and went to see who was there before they woke Sarah. Mia cracked the door open to find Tracy on the other side, holding a tray of medications.

"Hey, Mia. Sarah needs to take her meds. Is she awake?"

"I'm not sure. She's probably still sleeping, but you're more than welcome to check."

Tracy shook her head and handed over the tray to Mia. "You can give her the tray. She knows what to take and how to take them. She always gives me a fight, so it's your turn today." She laughed and headed back down the hallway. "Come find me if you need anything else!"

Mia sighed. She walked over to Sarah's bedroom and peeked inside. She saw the outline of Sarah's body wrapped in a blanket.

"You do a horrible job of being quiet," Sarah muttered from the darkness.

"I didn't know you were awake. Tracy came to give you your medications. I'll leave it there on the nightstand."

"Is it those damn blue and black pills?"

"No, these are yellow, red, and clear pills."

"Oh, that's the good stuff! Bring the tray in here." Mia pushed the door open with her foot and sat herself and the tray down beside Sarah. One by one, Sarah took the pills, finishing with a smile. "Those blue and black ones are the ones that make me feel bad. I hate those damn pills."

"What are those pills supposed to help with?"

"Why do you care? Leave it be."

Mia stood up to leave the room, but Sarah reached out and grabbed her wrist, trying to pull her back towards the bed.

"What's wrong?" Mia gasped, startled by Sarah's quick move.

"Sit." The firmness in her voice let Mia know Sarah was not playing around and she did as she was told.

"Don't you want me to turn the lights on?" asked Mia.

"No. I like it dark." Sarah took a few moments to adjust herself in the bed. "I've been lying here for a while, staring at the walls. I've got a lot on my mind. I dozed off, and when I fell asleep, I saw you in a place that I can only visit in my dreams now. That place is private. It's sacred to me. I go there from time to time to sit and watch water flow from a quiet stream. I see her each time I go there, just as she was the last time I saw her. I laid my head in her lap as she rubbed my head and told me, '*It is well*.'"

"What happened in your dream? Did I do something wrong?" Mia asked, puzzled.

"No, but this time my dream was different. You were there by the stream with us. She kept repeating the word *Nitakupata*. I don't know what it all means." Sarah reached out and held onto Mia's hand. "I loved my husband and son, but never once did I see either one of them at that stream. Never once did I get the urge to tell them what it is I have to say. I kept quiet. I've always kept quiet. I never wanted anyone to tell me that she didn't exist or that her life wasn't real. I never wanted to see her get hurt, either. You're the first one who ever showed up, and that can't be by accident. I don't know how much longer I have on this earth, but I know that before I do pass, I need to tell someone about her. I'm ashamed even thinking about what I did, but here you are, annoying as hell but willing to listen, and that can't be by accident either."

"You can tell me anything. I promise you, whatever you tell me is safe with me."

"That's the problem," Sarah said, sighing. "I should never have kept her story a secret in the first place. She never wanted it that way. She wanted me to tell the truth, to tell the world about what she went through, and I failed her."

"Who are you talking about? Who is she?"

A few deep breaths pushed her closer to the edge of the cliff. There was nowhere to run anymore. Vulnerability tasted sour, causing Sarah's tongue to twist and curl in her mouth, but she had to allow Mia in if she would ever find peace. In that rare moment, she was clear-minded and alert. There would not be a better time to start.

"I guess the best place to start is at the beginning. I'll tell you everything about my life before I met her so you can understand why things happened the way they did. So, listen closely and don't interrupt me!"

CHAPTER THIRTEEN

NORMAL

"These memories of mine don't always cooperate. They're scattered around the floor of my mind like pieces of a discarded puzzle. Some here and others there. People, different faces, and names, all fading with every minute. I don't mind losing those memories that don't serve me any purpose, ones that aren't even outlined in color anymore. It's memories, like those of my mother, that I try to hide in a safe place. Trying my best not to let them slip away like everything else that is starting to fade. You would've loved her. Everyone did. Her name was Ruth. A beautiful, strong name that matched my momma's spirit. I remember her brown eyes that captivated me every time they grabbed mine and held me there until she looked away. Her petite figure made it hard for men not to stare and women not to get jealous. I remember her beautiful black hair, always pinned up, always neat and presentable. She was the epitome of what a lady should be.

"I remember the sad times when I would wake to hear her crying. An unbearable pain she must've felt from my poppa and her brother dying in the war. I remember our home in Norfolk. It was small, but we loved it and stayed because my poppa built that small wooden house with his bare hands. I remember the times my momma made me feel loved, like

when she held my hand to lift me up to drink from fountains that said, 'for colored only'. I remember trips to the ocean, ice cream falling on hot cement, and walks in the park together on cool fall days. She did her best to shelter me from anyone who wanted to hurt me. Because of her love, I never really knew the world's cruelty towards colored people. Those parts of my childhood and days that just fell in line, one-by-one, are now left lingering with her sweet scent.

"I learned my numbers and letters, went to school, and wanted to become a teacher as early as I can remember. I wanted to make my momma proud. I was normal, and that's where I was content. Momma loved my normal. Normal was where I belonged. Then, I turned sixteen... and my normal life was shattered.

"I came home from school one day to find Momma on the floor. A cough she had come down with got heavier, and her whole body gave out on her that day. The doctor said she was sicker than what he could treat, and after that day, she never walked again. I wanted to quit school and go find a job, but Momma forbade it. She was making a good living washing clothes for people, mostly well-to-do black and white people around town. She made a good name for herself and wanted to ensure I kept the business going while she was on 'bed rest.' She refused to let her illness get the best of her. From her bed, she taught me everything she could about washing clothes, how to clean stubborn stains, and how to speak to her white customers. She did such a great job washing rich white folks' linens; they would travel across town to have her wash the piss and dirt off their sheets. Washing those piss-stained sheets kept us from knowing the hell the Depression could cause a family.

"So, every day after school, I would drop my books at the door and get right to work—washing, scrubbing, wringing, and hanging. I tried my best to keep up with her workload, but one by one, they stopped coming, knowing Momma wasn't the one doing the good work anymore.

I became worried every day that we would go hungry, but God was good to us, and we never did.

"Two years passed, and Momma kept declining. I graduated from school and made Momma as proud as she could be. That was the last time I ever saw her radiant smile. She took her last breath on a cold Tuesday morning. We had a service and buried her in the church cemetery, next to a makeshift plot we made for Poppa. I dressed her in her favorite purple and white dress. I sat in that little house, alone, crying for days. She wasn't there to protect or love me anymore.

"I think it was about a week or so after Momma passed that I was still in a state of depression when my friend, Claudette, came to the house to see how I was doing. Momma used to tell me that Claudette was one of those "passing" girls; they could marry a white or black man and get away with choosing either side. Back then, her slender figure and fair face made her the object of every boy's eye. She used to flick those light brown curls of hers around just to taunt and tease them. Men were so overtaken by her that they didn't even notice that Claudette's eyes only sparkled and perked up when another woman walked into the room. We didn't talk about things like that back in my day, and Claudette never let anyone know her true nature while we were growing up. Luckily, I wasn't much to look at. She thought of me as nothing more than a friend, and that's the way I liked it.

"I wasn't up for talking or seeing anyone, but she didn't take no for an answer. She stayed a while, and as we were talking and trying to change the subject from Momma passing, she told me about a job opportunity she had recently gotten in Hampton. Honestly, I didn't care, but I tried to be a good friend and congratulated her on her new job. She gave me a look, and that's when she asked if I wouldn't mind doing her a favor. A huge favor, from what she said. Even though I was short on favors, I told her I would help. She was my best friend, so I felt as though I didn't have a choice.

"She went on to tell me that the Hampton Institute recruited some educated Black men and women to help with the development of a Virginia Negro Studies Project that was a part of the Federal Writers' Project under the Works Progress Administration. It was a part of Roosevelt's 'New Deal.' I learned about bits and pieces of it from the newspapers that I salvaged from street corners. President Roosevelt was giving people a much-needed sense of hope from the pain of the Depression by creating jobs and other opportunities. She and the rest of the group were tasked with finding and collecting first-hand accounts, songs, and other narratives from formerly enslaved people. I looked at her as soon as she said the word 'enslaved.' Slaves? I had no idea what I was getting myself into, but she assured me she'd give me a cut of her pay for helping her, and that was enough for me. I was down to only two customers left who came to get their linens washed. I knew they would soon find someone else to take their business to. She promised she'd be back in a few days after she got approval to make sure I could come help her out. I was secretly hoping she wouldn't need my help after all, but there she was at my door a few days later, dragging me off to that Institute.

"I don't remember much of what they told me. I just recall that we were told to go around the surrounding areas to interview anyone we could find. The Project wanted to collect their way of life, songs, and other history while they were enslaved. They shared the project's mission, as well as tips on finding and speaking to anyone who lived during or before the Civil War. The rest of the group dispersed, leaving me and Claudette assigned to a smaller group with a few other people.

"I wasn't sure if the project was for me. It seemed like a lot of footwork and wasted hours trying to find a needle in a haystack. I walked over to Claudette and told her I made a mistake. I didn't want to help anymore; I wanted to go home. She pulled me aside and begged me to stay. She said she was having the worst luck finding people who would talk to her.

Claudette was adamant about her theory that two heads were better than one. Her tears pulled on my heart and I agreed to stay. She said we would be taking a ride out to the James City County area just outside of Williamsburg. That's where some people agreed to speak with the group that day. I had nothing to lose at that point. I agreed and found myself pressed up against Claudette and others in our group on the back of an old Ford pickup truck. It was driven by a white man who was a friend of one of the instructors, just in case we ran into any problems heading up the road. I tried my best to clear my mind, letting my freshly pressed hair dance in the cool morning air of that fateful day.

"We finally arrived at the home of our group lead. He was a tall, handsome black man named Joseph. He told us all to call him Joe. We traveled far away from the busy streets of the city and into a rural area full of thick, budding trees and hidden rocky dirt roads. We were all going to stay at Joe's parents' house, then return to Hampton. He gave everyone their assignments, and we all said our farewells and headed in our respective directions. I was walking off with Claudette, but Joe pulled me aside just as we were leaving. He apologized for his abrupt pull of my arm and told me he wanted me to try speaking to an old woman up the road, named Lucinda. She was known around town for being mean and scared off everyone in the group. He wanted me to give it a shot by trying to collect her story. I was hesitant and didn't want to be alone in a place I'd never been before, especially with a woman everyone feared. Claudette looked at me and told me to give it a try. She was scared off by the old woman, too. They both assured me that Lucinda was harmless and Claudette promised to walk me right up to Lucinda's door.

"Fortunately, we didn't have a long way to walk. Joe walked with us about half a mile up the main gravel road and onto one of those hidden dirt roads. Tree limbs hung down onto the path we were to walk through. All I could see were thick white spiderwebs and other creepy insects, all waiting to become entangled in my thick hair. He lifted some of the

branches and pointed up the dirt road, reminding Claudette of where to go to find the old woman. I gripped her hand, praying to God every step of the way."

CHAPTER FOURTEEN

INTERRUPTED

"I'm not boring you, am I?" said Sarah, pausing her story.

"No, ma'am, I want to know more. What happened? Did you meet Lucinda?" Mia was eager to hear more, sitting anxiously on the edge of the bed.

Sarah was about to begin her story again when she paused, looking around the room, puzzled. "What in the world is that noise?"

Mia was so engrossed in Sarah's story that she didn't hear the muffled buzzing noise in the next room. She ignored it until she realized it was her cell phone going off in her purse. Mia told Sarah to continue, but she refused. The phone continued to vibrate, annoying Sarah.

Buzzz. Buzzz. Buzzz.

Mia walked out to grab her purse.

"I'm going to go out and take this. I'm sorry."

Sarah shooed Mia away. Mia sighed, stepping out into the empty hallway.

"Hello?" Mia answered happily. She was so elated that she had neglected to see who was calling.

"Mia?! Finally! You've got some explaining to do, young lady. I've been all over the city looking for you! Where in God's name are you?!"

"I'm fine," Mia groaned, as her entire body slumped over in disgust at the sound of her mother's voice. "I'm in Virginia."

"Virginia? Why Virginia?"

"I've been here since the meeting at the lawyer's office. I'm spending time with *my* grandmother."

"David's mother?"

"Yes. She has been telling me all about her and my dad. I can't go into detail right now. Sarah's waiting for me."

"Mia, you've done nothing but disrespect me since you barged into my home. You come in yelling at me, slamming my door, ignoring my phone calls, and now brushing me aside for a stranger." Norma went on scolding Mia, but her words fell on deaf ears. Mia pressed her back to the door of Sarah's room, pulled the phone away from her ear, and allowed Norma to continue her rant into the air of the empty hallway. She hadn't had a panic attack since she arrived in Virginia, and there was no way she was going to let Norma break her streak of good mental health. Mia continued waiting patiently for the sweet sound of silence from the other end of the phone. She hoped Norma would hang up, but she could still hear her breathing on the other end.

"Sarah's waiting for me. I have to go," she whispered back into the phone.

"Did you even hear a word I said? I said, what about your job, Mia?"

"I'm going back to work in a few days. Mr. Garner is fully aware of what's going on, and I don't want to talk about it anymore. I'll call you when I leave Virginia. Don't worry about me. I'm fine. Have a good day, Norma."

Mia hung up the phone before her mother could respond. She placed the phone on silent and went back to Sarah's bedside.

"What the hell was that, making all that noise?"

"That was my mother calling. I haven't spoken to her since I left New York."

"Oh, well, are you planning on leaving?"

"I'm not going anywhere. You said you have something you need to tell me, so I'm not going anywhere."

"Good. That's good."

"Go on," Mia said, "tell me about Lucinda."

CHAPTER FIFTEEN

ACCEPTED

"Instantly, regret washed over me. What was I doing there with Claudette? What did I know about slaves other than what teachers taught me? I wasn't prepared for what was up that dirt road.

"Claudette and I did our best to keep the spiderwebs and thick leaves from touching our freshly pressed hair. I remember the small, jagged pebbles that got stuck in my shoes along the way. I held her hand tight, terrified at the sounds of snapping twigs made by rummaging squirrels off in the distance. All I could think about was my momma. I pressed my shaking hand to my cheek and remembered her soft touch. Her touch always made me feel loved and calmed my fears. I kept my hand pressed firmly into my face the rest of the way.

"Through the heavy tree branches and thick foliage, once again, the sunlight found us in a small clearing. No bigger than my backyard back home stood a secluded wooden cabin. The roof was covered in overgrown moss that was darkened with shades of green and gray. There were broken tree limbs scattered all across the roof, surrounding the ground. The cabin's wood was dilapidated and rotting on all of its sides, but somehow still looked sturdy. Holes in the wood were patched with wet mud and dry leaves. There was a black chimney pipe coming out of the

roof. I could see thick gray smoke rising into the air. Seeing the isolated cabin made me want to turn around and run. I could tell from the way the cabin was hidden that Lucinda did not care much for guests. It was evident she wanted to keep the world out.

"As we made our way to the cabin's front door, I started thinking. A few weeks ago, my life was normal. I had my momma and I was happy. Now, my normal disappeared, and I found myself walking to a stranger's doorstep. I was scared to death, knowing I needed to ask her to share with me a time in her life she probably never wanted to relive.

"Claudette knocked softly on the old wooden door and took a few steps back. I must have still been buried in my thoughts because I didn't hear her warning me to move away. Just as her hand caught the belt of my skirt and tugged me backward, the door flew open, and a splash of icy water struck my face. I gasped, choking as it soaked into my hair and clothes, and stumbled back, my heels scraping the ground as I fought to keep my balance. For a split second, I didn't know where I was or what had happened. I wiped frantically at my eyes, water dripping from my lashes as I tried to see who had done it. A figure loomed in the doorway, framed by the open door, and from inside came a deep, raspy voice wrapped in a thick Southern accent. She spoke slowly, deliberately, her words heavy with irritation.

"'Y'all chillun back on my doorstep?! I told y'all I ain't got nothin' tuh say! I got ah good mind tuh get Ol' Ben!'

"Claudette pushed me behind her and began pleading her case. I finally got my sight back and peered around Claudette's shoulders to get a better look at her. She was a small, fragile old woman, no bigger than a growing teenager. I remember the red cloth head wrap that sat on her head, all twisted and tucked in place. She wore a tattered plaid pioneer-looking dress with an apron tied to her skinny little waist. Her skin was still rich with a tone of mahogany brown. Her big eyes, staring angrily at me, were the color of fresh bark on the trees surrounding us.

"Claudette's pleading was getting us nowhere. Lucinda still stood firm, demanding that we leave. Realizing the seriousness in her voice, I quickly blurted out what I could to keep her from slamming the door in our faces. I pushed past Claudette, taking a few steps closer to Lucinda. I felt my momma's hand on my cheek again as I told her my name was Sarah. I stumbled through my words, trying to let her know we meant her no harm. I don't remember exactly what I said; I just know I begged her to give me a chance to talk to her. I'd come so far and needed the money so bad that tears started to swell in the corners of my eyes. She said nothing. I was sure she was seconds from slamming the door in my face. I slowly dropped my head in defeat, letting the greasy drops of water roll down my face.

"She looked me up and down at first. I didn't know what to expect from her. I stood there, waiting for her next move. She finally gave a little chuckle and signaled for me to come in. I couldn't believe it. I could hear Claudette behind me moving towards the door, too. Lucinda tossed her hand up in the air, stopping Claudette in her tracks.

"'Only one of y'all comin' in. Go on an' get! She fine here wit me.'

"I paused at the door, seeing Claudette turn with a huge smile on her face. I was granted access, and she was thrilled, even though she was forced to leave.

"'I'll meet you down the road at dusk!' she called out to me and waved goodbye."

CHAPTER SIXTEEN

FADING

"You must've been scared, Sadie. Going into a stranger's house like that."

"You have no idea, child. Felt like nothing I'd ever experienced before."

"Why do you think she chose you instead of Claudette?" Sarah took a few moments, letting her eyes wander around the dimly lit bedroom.

"I truly have no idea why. I still, to this day, can't grasp why she chose me out of all those people who came to her doorstep. I wasn't much to look at, and I surely wasn't college-educated like the others in the group. But there I was, standing in that old cabin, scared to death of what she was going to do next."

"My best friend, Bee, says everything happens for a reason. She is into astrology, spiritual numbers, and that kinda stuff."

"What do you believe in?" Sarah asked.

"Well, I believe in God. I believe everything happens for a reason, too, just not the magical way she sometimes makes it out to be."

"Well, I'm just glad you believe in something."

"I hate to get off topic, but I have to ask. Claudette sounds like a really good friend. Do you two still keep in touch?"

Sarah chuckled sarcastically at Mia's question. "I believe we would if she wasn't dead."

"Oh, no!" Mia gasped. "I'm so sorry, Sadie. I didn't mean to—"

Sarah patted Mia on the knee and sighed. "Child, she died decades ago. She got caught up in a life she couldn't handle. Drugs got a hold of her, and her 'lady friend' called me one day to tell me she overdosed."

Mia was silent. She couldn't understand how Sarah was so calm after losing such a close friend. Tears welled up in her eyes thinking about losing Bee.

Sarah could tell that the hard truth hit a soft spot in Mia's heart. Part of her wanted to scold Mia for being so naïve. Sarah remembered her first spat with death, seeing her uncle laid out in a casket. She then recalled the day she found her mother with closed eyes and cold skin. Sarah decided that a harsh recourse wouldn't be helpful at that moment. Mia's tender age hadn't exposed her to everything Sarah had endured. She had to respect that. She set aside her feelings of discontent and gave Mia the kindest reality check she could.

"Child, look at me. I'm almost ninety years old. Why would you think I haven't seen my fair share of death? It has become a part of me. Everyone I've ever loved is now dead and gone. My dear friend Claudette is no exception. You only know death through David's passing, I'm sure. Try losing everyone you love. Then you'll see how numb it makes you inside."

"Not having him in my life did something to me. I hate death now," Mia pouted, wiping her eyes. "I hate seeing it and hearing about it. Makes me want to curl into a ball and hide."

"No hiding from it, child. It's coming for all of us one day, I can promise you that."

Mia sighed and tried to change the conversation. "Are you getting tired at all, Sadie?" Mia asked, placing her hand on top of Sarah's.

"No. I'm fine. I might need to get a little rest soon, but I can see her clear as day right now and I don't want to lose this moment. Moments like this don't happen much for me anymore. I want to keep going."

"I understand." Mia nodded. "Please go on."

CHAPTER SEVENTEEN

STEADFAST

"I stayed put, cautious of her every move. I was scared of more water being thrown at me. I watched as she paced throughout the cabin. She was old, but her steps were far from feeble. She didn't slouch or have a bend in her back like other old people I'd seen trying to walk. I could tell right away she was different. The old wooden floorboards made deep, cracking noises as she passed over them. Lucinda knew her space intimately, stepping lightly across the room, knowing which boards to avoid to keep the space quiet. She said nothing at first. She went back to what she was doing before we knocked, which was adding firewood to the small cast-iron stove. Heat radiated into the spaces of the cabin, which helped to dry the last drops of water from my dampened hair.

"Her silence gave me time to look around the room. The cabin had no bedrooms or bathroom inside, just one open space that held everything she owned. Scorched metal pots and pans hung from hooks on the wooden walls. Off in one corner was a small, makeshift bed with pieces of hay sticking out from every direction. Shaded sunlight peeked through the glass of the two windows on opposite sides of the cabin. An old gasoline lamp that hung by the back door made a soft clinking sound every time Lucinda stepped through the cabin.

Close by sat a large, beautifully decorated yellow-and-white porcelain washbowl with a matching white pitcher inside. The bowl sat on top of a pile of discarded books covered in thick layers of dust. I could smell fresh lye soap coming from damp cotton dresses that were hanging from a long string of twine.

"I was standing still for so long; I was sure she had forgotten I was there. I became more intrigued with every step she made. Intrigued by this woman's experience as a slave, I couldn't believe this was a person who'd been through things that my generation only read about in stories and history books. I was fascinated by her, and I didn't even know her. She finally turned to me with a look of disappointment in her eyes.

"'Y'all ain't got no shame. Why in God's name do y'all keep pesterin' me? Ain't nobody cared one lick 'bout me an' my life. Now here ya an' the rest of dem nosey chillun come knockin' an' askin' me for my past like it's sweets I got ready tuh share. Ya look like ya got some sense, so why ya here?'

"Her strong, raspy voice cut into me like a knife. I stood there, soaked in embarrassment. I didn't know what to say at first. She was right. What right did I or any of the others have coming here? Asking her for her story like it was some casual conversation between friends? I didn't think about what bad memories it would bring or how it would make her feel to divulge the hurt strapped to her back. All I knew was that I needed the money, and I didn't want to go back home empty-handed. But I couldn't tell her that. I couldn't be that heartless.

"I expressed again why I was there and that I didn't want to cause any trouble. She let me finish my side of things, eyeing me up and down with every word that came stumbling out of my mouth. I kept my eyes looking towards the floor just in case she wanted to throw more water my way. After I finished with what I had to say, she went to a corner of the room and grabbed a large pot from the wall. She walked over and dropped it in front of me, and damn near dropped it on my toes! Her eyes

looked a little less disappointed and a little more determined. She pointed to the pot and that deep, raspy voice started up again.

"'I's sick of y'all comin' here an' botherin' me. Done chasin' y'all away. Gettin' old an' I ain't gonna keep dat up. Ol' Ben don't even chase like he used tuh. I's decided not tuh waste this here good breath I got. I's gonna make ya work. Ya gonna earn my words. Nothin' 'bout my story free. I need help 'round here. Take dat there pot an' go fill it up in dat stream out back. I got carrots tuh boil. Then ya gonna pick dem weeds comin' up out my floor. Don't fret, got plenty more after dat's done.'

"What could I say? I felt as though I had no choice but to do what she said. She walked over to the back door of the cabin. It creaked and moaned as she pushed it open for me. My eyes became fixed on a small, beautiful garden hiding behind that rickety old house. There were rows of budding flowers, plants, and root vegetables everywhere. I could see a small stream flowing just beyond the garden, quietly trickling water back into the thick woods. The smell of fresh mint and lavender floated in the air, overtaking my senses.

"'Be careful,' she called out to me, 'Ol' Ben don't take kindly tuh strangers.'

"She pointed over to a chicken coop. Surrounding it were a few plump-looking hens that quietly pecked for the feed scattered around the dirt. Off to the side, I caught sight of a big mean-looking devil with red and black feathers sticking straight up out of its head. I had no doubt that the evil-looking rooster was Ol' Ben. He looked straight at me and started flapping his wings like crazy, looking as if he wanted to fight me. Lucinda gave three loud clicks from the roof of her mouth. Ol' Ben stopped flapping his wings and went back under the coop, now unbothered by my presence.

"'He calm now. Go on an' fill dat pot.'

"It took hours for me to complete everything she wanted done that day. Except for her giving me new tasks to do, we didn't speak one word

while I was working. She sat in an old chair by the door, watching me go back and forth throughout her cabin. I finally finished the last few tasks, which were pulling, washing, and peeling the carrots. I knew I had to get back to the main road soon to meet Claudette. I got a little discouraged watching that sun go down. I knew I hadn't gotten what I'd come there for, and Claudette was counting on me. I was counting on that money. I didn't want to go back to her empty-handed.

"'Come back here by noon 'morrow. I got more work 'round here for ya.'

"I breathed a sigh of relief. I agreed to come back, afraid to say anything else but goodbye.

"I found Claudette waiting for me, as promised. I told her about what happened with Lucinda. She gave me a look of doubt. Once back at Joe's house, she called everyone over to have me retell my day with Lucinda. They all acted as if I performed a miracle like Jesus, changed water into wine or healed the blind. One girl asked me, 'How did you do it?' Another one patted my back and said, 'She chased me away with a broom when I went to see her last week! She was mean as bull spit!'

"'She threw a stick at me!' Joe laughed. 'Told me never to come back, and I didn't!' I chuckled at their attempts but assured them that Lucinda was not welcoming at first. I told them how she splashed me with water and showed them my frizzy hair that was once perfectly pressed. I told them how she made me peel carrots, move mossy firewood, and clean weeds from the floor, but surprisingly, she told me to come back the next day.

"I turned down for the night, feeling good about myself, but as the night went on and I began to toss and turn, those feelings started to change. I began to feel like I made the biggest mistake of my life going there. I felt like an ant and Lucinda's shoe was hovering over my head that night as I slept. How insignificant I felt coming there to gain her trust and get her story, not really caring about anything she could possibly tell

me. I was there because Claudette asked me to come, not because I was interested in the Project or getting slave stories recorded. I simply wanted to help my friend get Lucinda's story and get the money for doing so. It terrified me to think that Lucinda might find out my real motives, that her past and memories were pointless to someone like me. I was terrified she'd find out who I really was."

CHAPTER EIGHTEEN

INTERMISSION

Sarah paused for a few moments. Recalling her memories of Lucinda took a toll on her. Mia could hear the exhaustion building up in Sarah's voice. Her words had become more spaced apart, and she could see her eyes drooping in the faint light of the room.

"I need to rest a while," muttered Sarah. "I need a little time to build my strength back up, that's all. Then we can go to dinner. I think it's spaghetti night, and I don't want you making me miss spaghetti night!" Sarah patted Mia on the hand and shooed her away. Mia stood and left the room so Sarah could rest. She called out to Mia to give her an hour, then she'd begin her story again.

Mia decided to use the break wisely. She grabbed her phone from her purse and walked out into the hallway, careful not to disturb Sarah while she slept. A smile stretched across her face as she saw only messages and calls from Bee. Mia felt a sense of victory when Norma retreated and left her alone. Mia punched in Bee's number and walked over to a chair in the hallway. Before Bee could even say hello, Mia was blurting out hurried sentences that made no sense to Bee.

"Mia! Mia! Slow down! What on earth is going on with you?"

Mia realized her voice was echoing through the empty hallway and dropped to a low whisper to avoid disturbing the other residents.

"I'm so excited, Bee! I'm sorry. I can't help it! I'm here in Virginia with Sarah, my grandmother! She's talking to me and letting me know all about her past. I'm so excited!"

"Yeah, I can tell! Well, start from the beginning and don't leave anything out."

Mia tried to get her giddiness under control. She took a few deep breaths and went to the beginning, first telling Bee about the lawyer's office and everyone she had met, including her father's rude wife, Valerie. She moved on to her first encounter with Sarah, and how she jumped over hurdles just to spend time with her. She now sat listening to Sarah's past and the freed woman named Lucinda. Mia tried to leave nothing unturned, giving all the details she could remember. She finished the story with her heroic moment of hanging up on Norma.

"Wow, you hung up on her?" Bee said, shocked that Mia was so bold.

"Yes, I did and I'm proud that I did. She has been calling me non-stop since I left her house. I was calm and didn't disrespect her, but she had to go. Honestly, I don't know if I will ever talk to her again."

"I would understand if you didn't, but she's your mom, Mia, no matter how much you hate her."

"I don't hate her," Mia replied. "I'll talk to her eventually. It won't be anytime soon, though." Mia went on telling Bee all about the nursing home and anything else she could think of. Pretty soon, she looked at her phone to see that an hour had gone by.

"Bee, I gotta go. Sarah should be awake now, and she has to finish her story."

"Okay, just promise me you'll be home for my birthday."

"I promise. I'll call you soon, I promise."

With that, the two friends said goodbye, and Mia hurried back to the room. She poked her head into Sarah's dark bedroom, softly knocking on the side of the door.

"I'm up, child. Come sit down." Mia went to her spot on the edge of Sarah's bed. She spotted some balled-up pieces of Kleenex tissue around Sarah that weren't there before. Mia was puzzled. *Was Sarah... crying?*

"Sarah, is everything okay?" she asked.

"You'll have to forgive me," Sarah mumbled with guilt. "I've been sitting here trying to remember what happened with Lucinda. It's getting blurry. I think I can finish, though, but I can only tell you what memories decide to come back."

"We don't have to keep going. I'm not in a rush. Like you said before, it's getting close to dinnertime anyway. We can stop and go eat."

"No!" Sarah shouted, startling Mia. "I have to finish!"

Mia sat still, allowing Sarah to retrieve her fading memories.

CHAPTER NINETEEN

HEAVY

"I was a bit more optimistic by the next morning. I walked up that dirt road, certain Lucinda would give me words to cover the blank sheets of paper I carried with me. She opened her door and looked at the paper in my hand and the eager smile stretched across my face. She folded her arms and grunted, amused at the idea that I gained her trust.

"She put me in the garden that day. It was just my luck that the sun decided to come out, hot and heavy. She put me out there in that heat to test me, I'm sure of it. She kept her eyes on me, assessing my every move. I tugged and pulled deep-rooted weeds that had become tangled alongside the vegetables. Sweat rolled down my temples as the sun found a resting place on my forehead. I was relieved when it fell behind the thick shade of the trees. I stopped in the moments I knew she turned her back to me to quickly smell the tips of lavender that brushed up against my wet face.

"She then called out to me from inside the cabin to uproot a few ripened vegetables. I grabbed two heavy sweet potatoes and some plump carrots from the soil. I brushed them off as best I could and placed them into the pockets of the apron Lucinda had tied on me.

"'Ya show fool me, gal,' she called out to me from the doorway, 'Ya looks tuh be one of dem uppity negro gals, but ya got the back of ah' fieldhand!'

"'I used to help my momma out with washing heavy sheets and blankets. It doesn't bother me much.' I paused for a few moments, wiping the sweat away from my forehead.

"'Well, keep at it. Hand me dat an' go get ah few eggs from dat coop. Ol' Ben ain't up for chasin' today so ya safe. Best I feed ya now. Ya sweatin' an' need somethin' in dat belly.'

"I handed her the heavy vegetables and thanked her for her kindness. I made my way to the chicken coop, with Ol' Ben under the wooden steps, eyeing me up and down. He had it out for me. I could feel it. He was waiting for the right time to peck my eyes out! His red and black feathers were calm as I tiptoed up to the coop. He sat there in the shade, avoiding me and the sun. I grabbed what I needed from inside the coop and shuffled quickly back into the house.

"Lucinda got to work boiling the vegetables and eggs. I washed my hands in the porcelain bowl, trying my best to get the dirt and chicken feathers from under my fingernails. I sat down on the floor beside her chair and crossed my legs like my momma taught me to do. I sat quietly as a mouse, patiently waiting for my portion of food. She moved and shuffled around that hot stove like it was nothing to her. The heat in the cabin made my armpits drip more sweat, but I was too busy watching her to notice it soaking through my clothes.

"She reached over and pulled a few pieces of sweetbread from a small metal box near the stove. Her eyes pressed shut as she brought the bread close to her nose and took in a deep breath of its buttery corners.

"'Dis' here be duh best sweetbread in Virginia! Mattie always make good on dat recipe! Taste just like Bess' sweetbread. Bess be proud.' Lucinda took a few bites of the bread and laughed.

"'Who's Mattie?' I asked, licking my lips at the sight of moist bread crumbs falling from her mouth.

"'Mattie freed, like me. Lives ah few miles up dat road. Comes through here tuh see her kin. Sweetest woman I know 'sides my Mary. Stops by tuh share dat prize-winnin' sweetbread. I give her what I got from my garden an' she be kind tuh give me spices, twine an' dis here sweetbread.'

Lucinda took another bite of the sweetbread. She finally finished plating the food and made her way over to her chair.

"'Eat.' She huffed, pushing the tin plate of steaming food and sweetbread towards me. I took one look at the plate and dove in. She chuckled, watching me eat as though I'd never been given a drop of food in my life until that day.

"'Ya say yo' name Sarah?'

"'Yes ma'am. Sarah Bishop.' My head stayed down as I shoved the food in my mouth.

"'So, Sarah Bishop, ya doin' all dat work out there an' sweatin' like ah' ox, just cuz ya needin' my story?'

"I tried my best to answer her through the boiled egg stuffed in my mouth. 'My friend, Claudette, needs my help with collecting stories for her school. Slave stories, like yours. You wouldn't talk to her, so she wanted me to come try to talk to you instead.'

"'I ain't reckon anyone 'round here wantin' tuh know what I got tuh say.'

"'They say it's important that we collect your story because it's a part of history.' I kept my eyes down, making sure that I got every drop of food into my mouth. She watched me as I ate, looking unamused. I was surprised when she lifted her hand and placed it on my head, running her fingers through a few strands of hair that came loose from my pinned-up bun.

"'I seen dat hair God give tuh ya when I splashed ya yesterday. Ah' little water cure anythin'. Ya come back here all pressed an' proper, I see.'

"She flicked one of the strands in my face and released a disappointed grunt. I took pride in my hair and the fact that I stayed up that night, pressing my hair, trying my best to look presentable to her. She didn't see it that way. She grabbed my shoulder and turned me around so that she could look me in the eyes.

"'Why yo' hair like this? Ya wanna be like ah white gal or somethin'?'

"I remember I was thrown off by her question. Of all the things she could've asked me, she went for my hair. I was polite and I said to her, "No ma'am. I like my hair straight. It's proper and neat. My momma told me that all proper women wear their hair straight and neat." She looked straight at me and laughed.

"'God ain't give no negro straight hair! I seen dat kinky hair come out moment dat water touched it. Kinked up real good! But here ya come, back tuh my home, an' it's done got straight again. Why? Ya don't like yo'self? Ya don't love dat hair God give ya?'

"I felt insulted. How could she hint at the fact that I didn't love myself all because I straightened my hair? After she said what she said, I turned my back to her and went on finishing my food.

"Lucinda took a few moments and stood up from her chair. I was seconds from licking the rim of the tin plate when she reached down and grabbed it from my hands. She placed it on the seat of her chair and began unraveling her red head wrap. It was much longer than I imagined. It slowly wound down to the floor until her head was revealed to me. She stood there, proud and unashamed. Her head was as bald as a baby bird, with a few patches of fuzz scattered here and there. I gasped at the sight of her, but she didn't flinch.

"'The story dat ya come for be all in pieces. One piece be where my hair used tuh be. Ya got no idea the price I done paid for my story. Ya shamed of yo' thick God-given hair. Put fire in it all cuz white folk say ya

look better dat way. My hair cut from my head, all cuz white folk say I look better dis way. Only difference 'tween us is ya gots ah choice. Ain't many choices for me in my story.'

"I don't know what I could've said in that moment to make me feel less of an ass. She picked up the red head wrap from the floor and began circling it back around her head until it was once again secure. I looked up at her with tears in my eyes, ashamed of my ignorance.

"Lucinda walked towards the back door and nodded to me to follow her. I slowly stood up, brushed the crumbs from my legs, and followed her out towards the stream. She bent down and placed the tin plates into the flowing water, using her hands to wipe away the leftover pieces of food. She looked up at me, signaling for me to take over. Even though the heat was heavy that day, the water still ran cold. She stood over me, watching me until I was finished.

"'Stay put,' she instructed while she went and grabbed some linens from inside the cabin. 'Since you like washin', wash these here linens.'

"She handed me the clothes and a small piece of soap and retreated back to her chair in the cabin. I said nothing. I thought I was making some progress getting through to her, but I was certain my ignorance set me back. I scrubbed the linens with my hands and rung them until the cold water stopped dripping. I looked at my fingers, now wrinkled and stiff.

"'Come on an' hang dem on dis here line. Ya gots more work waitin', Miss Sarah Bishop.'"

CHAPTER TWENTY

CAUSE

"I can't imagine what that must've felt like seeing her like that."

"I never did press my hair again after that day. Seeing her and hearing the pain in her voice did something to me. It shook me right down to my core." Sarah gripped the bed sheet and twisted it between her fingers. "I believe that's the moment when the money no longer meant anything to me. Whatever selfish motive I had to be there with her disappeared. I wanted to know who she was. Maybe even get a glimpse of how to be as strong as her."

"No wonder you hate my wig. I know you must hate that I don't appreciate my real hair," Mia said.

"I don't hate anything about you, child. You don't know any better. You don't know your God-given beauty."

"I've never really considered myself beautiful."

"You can't be that dumb, child. You don't see how beautiful your hair is?"

"No ma'am. I always got teased about my hair. People always made jokes that it was nappy or dirty. I decided it was better if I just put wigs on to make people leave me alone. Plus, my best friend says

I dress like a dorky, depressed white girl. It's pretty pitiful when you think about it."

"Well, I can't argue with you on that."

"I want to see what you and Bee see in my hair, or anything about me, for that matter. I want to so bad. I never had anyone tell me these things, and I could never look to my mom for guidance."

"Well, stop blaming your momma or anyone for what's going on with you. You've done what a lot of people do and let sadness shape who you are. But you better stop, and you better stop right now. Nobody else is going to do it for you. It's called *self-love* for a reason. Hell, I'm old as dirt, and I know I look damn good! I earned this gray hair, and I'll never let anyone take that away from me!" Sarah playfully slapped the side of Mia's arm.

"I have to admit, taking off my wig and just being me for a change feels really good. It feels good not to have to be ashamed," Mia said.

"You wear that hair of yours out and be proud, child. Do it for women like Lucinda who never had a choice." Mia took a deep breath in as Sarah reached out and rubbed the side of her face with her palm. Mia could feel the wrinkles in Sarah's hand press into her face, and she melted in her grandmother's touch. Mia felt tears building up in her eyes again, and she quickly changed the subject to avoid losing Sarah to a moment of vulnerability.

"Did Lucinda finally tell you, her story? Did she tell you who did that to her?"

Sarah paused for a moment, then tapped Mia's hand. "I'm getting hungry. I need to eat."

Time had become the least of Mia's worries. She stood up, taking a glimpse of the clock perched on the wall outside the bedroom. She hadn't realized it was so late in the day.

"Do you want to go to the cafeteria again?" she asked.

"No, just push me to the kitchen table. They normally bring dinner around for us if we don't show up to the cafeteria."

Just as Mia was helping Sarah into her wheelchair, she heard a knock at the door. She pushed Sarah to the table and went to open the door, finding Tracy standing there with a smile and a cart full of food trays for dinner.

"Hi Mia. Didn't see you two at dinner. Sarah loves spaghetti night. I wouldn't want her to miss it. I have some spaghetti here for you too. I didn't have much else to dig up for you."

"That's fine!" Mia smiled, turning to close the door, but Tracy quickly placed her hand up, pushing it back open.

"Mia, please be sure she takes her medicine. It's very important that she does."

"What are they for?"

"They help with her memory and when she gets disoriented. Just helps to keep her calm. Can you make sure she takes them?"

"I will, no problem." Mia thanked Tracy again and closed the door. She took the trays to the table, watching as Sarah's face went from a stale smile to a twisted frown.

"What's wrong? Tracy said you loved spaghetti." Sarah pointed to a small white cup near her cup of apple juice, filled with blue and black pills.

"She put those damn pills I hate on there. I'm not going to take them. They make me feel funny. I don't want to take them."

"Sarah, you have to take your medication. You can't—"

"I can do whatever I want!" Sarah snapped. Mia decided it was best not to argue with Sarah. She shook her head and let Sarah begin eating. Mia didn't want to lose the good streak she was having. She could lose the chance to hear the rest of Sarah's story. Mia tried to change the subject, looking aimlessly around the room for something to talk about with Sarah. She landed on the paintings covering the walls, intrigued by the possibility of a story behind them, too.

"Those are some unique paintings, Sadie. Did you paint them?"

"My late husband, David's father, painted those. I love them. He was a terrible painter. He took up painting as a hobby before he died. They are dreadful to look at, but I love them anyway."

"What was my grandfather's name?"

"Joseph Newell, but I called him Joe."

"Wait. Is that the same Joe you met at the Institute?"

"Yep, that's the one. That's your grandaddy. He used to tell me he loved me ever since the day he laid eyes on me in that group meeting. He said I was the only one for him."

"That's beautiful!" Mia's heart melted at the rare thought of Sarah being vulnerable and having love for someone other than David.

"It's a crock of bull. I know he wanted Claudette first. She brushed him off faster than a fly on a hot dog. He was barking up the wrong tree, so he set his eyes on me instead. But I never made him feel bad about it, though. I know he loved me."

"I would love to know more about him, too. I could see them hanging in the museum I work at back home."

"I like them just fine here on my walls, thank you."

Mia continued inquiring about the eclectic items scattered throughout the room. She hoped to keep Sarah comfortable and get her in the mood to continue her story. She watched Sarah's handshake as she lifted it to point to each item in the room. Each memento had a story. Every knick-knack held a place in Sarah's heart. Sarah shared every detail clearly, remembering the day each item had somehow come into her possession. The two finished their meal, and Mia pushed Sarah back into her bedroom. She noticed as she was wheeling Sarah away that the pills that Sarah needed to take were still sitting on her tray. Mia again told herself not to interfere with Sarah's wishes and moved on.

"Do you feel up to telling me more about Lucinda?"

"No, you've talked my head off enough for today," scoffed Sarah, nestling herself under the covers.

Mia didn't argue. Her body and mind needed rest. It'd been a long day for both of them. She gently adjusted Sarah's pillows to ensure her comfort, then settled into the couch's crease, finding a comfortable spot to fall asleep.

CHAPTER TWENTY-ONE

EFFECT

Mia was awakened the next morning to the sound of the front door slamming shut. She caught sight of Sarah wheeling herself into the kitchen with her lap full of food. Mia rubbed her face and stood up from the couch to join Sarah at the kitchen table. She pressed her fingertips into her eyes, wiping away the sticky sleep that had formed in the corners.

"Good morning, Sadie," Mia whispered. "I would've gone to get you breakfast. Why didn't you ask me?"

"Just what in the hell do you think I was doing before you got here? Hmm? I'm not helpless, child. I can do things just fine. Here, go on and eat."

Mia sat down casually, ignoring Sarah's rudeness. She was used to her brazen comments and knew now when to speak and when to shut her mouth. She pulled a bear claw from the pile of sweets and took a few small bites of the cold pastry. The cool, fresh scent of potted mint leaves began to fill her nostrils. Several long, rejuvenating breaths helped to perk up her senses. She licked away some of the sweet almond slivers stuck to her fingers. Sarah was busy pulling apart an orange, not paying Mia any attention. Mia wiped her mouth and decided to try her luck again with Sarah's story.

"Sadie, I would love to hear more about Lucinda. What happened next?"

"Might as well finish what I started," Sarah huffed, wiping drops of orange juice from her lips. "You go get yourself together first in the bathroom. You look like hell. Can't tell my story if you're distracting me. Don't you turn on my bedroom light either. I like my room to stay dark!"

Mia nodded her head and did as she was told. She grabbed her bag from the couch and made her way to the bathroom.

Mia returned to the table, feeling at peace and relaxed after a hot shower and an outfit change. She kept her hair out and free. Her kinky coils bounced around, thankful for the chance to breathe. Mia placed her wig at the bottom of her bag to make sure it remained out of Sarah's sight.

"Now, where was I, child?"

"You stopped when Lucinda took off her head wrap and showed you her head."

"Yes, yes. Okay, I'll start there."

Sarah began with a few words, trying to start her story again. She rummaged through her mind to find the pieces to put everything back together. All she could do was draw a blank. The memories had vanished. She tried to shake it off and begin again, but still nothing. She was scared at what she could feel beginning to happen. It was moments like those that terrified her, moments when she could not remember things. Remember people or places that were once clear and vivid to her. She was standing there in her memory, looking into Lucinda's eyes. Remembering her tattered red headwrap, the smell of boiling sweet potatoes, and Ol' Ben shuffling around the backyard. Sarah began crying and softly tapping the side of her head, desperately trying to hold on to Lucinda and the invaluable memories she had of her.

"I can't remember. I can't remember!" Sarah repeated over and over. She was nervous and agitated. She started shaking and yelling at the top of her lungs.

"I can't remember! I can't lose her again! I can't lose her again! God, please!"

Mia jumped up, frightened by Sarah's sudden outburst. She tried to calm Sarah down, but Sarah kept yelling, growing increasingly restless. Mia rushed out the door, yelling for Tracy to come to the room. Luckily, Tracy was not far away when she heard Mia's cries for help and came running. Tracy rushed to Sarah's side, trying to console her.

"Sarah, it's alright. It's me, Tracy." Tracy began patting Sarah's back and calling out to her, but Sarah continued yelling, "I can't remember! I can't lose her again!"

Tracy gave Mia instructions on what to do and who to ask for help. Sarah's room soon filled with medical staff, who began working to calm her and bring her outbursts under control. Mia cried too. It all happened so fast. Sarah was fine one moment, then the next, she turned hysterical. Mia felt helpless to reach Sarah or understand why Sarah had broken down that way. She poked her head through the crowded doorway to see what was going on, but each time she was asked to leave the room. Mia had never felt so ashamed and powerless. She knew that she was solely to blame for Sarah's breakdown. All her questions and insisting that Sarah regurgitate her painful memories were too much. She stumbled into the empty chair in the hallway, watching her tears pool on the floor below her.

The noise around her started to fade. Mia's back stiffened with fear as she saw her helpless hands tremble and twitch. She tucked them between her thighs and began to rock back and forth. She knew it was only a matter of time before the darkness and muted black walls took control, but she needed to be strong. She bit down on the slippery flesh of her cheeks and watched for a sign of hope to emerge from the room.

Calm down, Mia. Please, calm down. Sarah is gonna be fine.

Nurses and other staff hurried past her, too busy to acknowledge her presence. In and out. In and out. Carts brushed by, squeaking under the weight of heavy, flashing medical equipment. Others brought in carts lined with various medications. She stared into each of the strangers' eyes, waiting to see that one familiar face, but there was no sign of Tracy.

The inward guilt of deliberately worsening Sarah's condition overwhelmed Mia. The burden pressed down on her as if she were sinking into the floor, a stark contrast to the relief she experienced with Sarah from the oppressive black walls and deafening silence. She cherished her brief freedom and dreaded returning to that dark place, yet the sensation of descending persisted. Her breathing strained, and her chest tightened. The clenched flesh of her cheek between her teeth released the metallic taste of blood in her mouth. Bowing her head, she watched the four thick walls close in around her.

CHAPTER TWENTY-TWO

REVELATION

The black walls slowly retreated as a warm hand pressed into Mia's shoulder. Mia slowly lifted her head, adjusting her eyes to see Tracy standing in front of her. She rubbed the tears from her guilt-stricken eyes, praying Tracy had good news for her.

"Mia, are you okay?" Tracy gently whispered. "I wanted to check on you. Why are you hunched over like that? Are you hurt?" Tracy frantically looked over Mia to make sure she was okay.

"I had another anxiety attack. I'm sorry, Tracy. I didn't mean to do this to her." Mia began crying again. Tracy crouched to Mia's eye level and handed her a tissue.

"Sarah's going to be fine, Mia. You did nothing wrong." Tracy's voice was calm and reassuring. "But there's something I need to talk to you about."

"Do you want me to leave?" Mia sniffled, trying to control her breathing. "I understand if you want me to leave."

"Oh no, nothing like that. You can stay. This isn't her first outburst, and it probably won't be the last. It wasn't major this time. There's nothing you did to cause it. I know how hard she fights to avoid taking her medication."

Mia was relieved to hear Tracy clear her of all wrongdoing. Tracy reached into her pocket and handed Mia more tissues. She stood up, reaching for Mia's hand.

"Let's go into the cafeteria. It's empty there, and we can have some privacy." Mia could tell from the look in Tracy's eyes that whatever she was going to say next wouldn't be something Mia wanted to hear. Tracy grabbed Mia some water, and the two sat down at an empty table.

"Did Sarah tell you about her condition?" Mia shook her head, unsure of what Sarah was hiding from her. "Yeah, I figured that. I thought Sarah would tell you, but I guess I was being too optimistic."

"What's going on with her? Is she dying?"

"She isn't at death's door yet, honey. She's a fighter and the toughest old woman I've had the pleasure of knowing. But she is sick and declining. Sarah was diagnosed with Alzheimer's disease. David cared for her, but it became too much for him and Valerie to handle, so when the city offered her a residence here, they were beyond grateful. She has her good days and her bad days, but she's probably never going to be fully back to normal."

"How long has she been like this?" Mia asked.

"For a few years now. She's mainly dealing with memory loss and really bad mood swings. She gets confused sometimes about places and things."

"There's nothing that can make her better?"

"There's no cure for what she has, honey. We're here to make her days as comfortable as possible now. We don't know how much longer she may have, but she isn't showing any signs of decline that would have us worried."

"Tracy, should I not push her anymore to tell me about her past? I know that's what triggered her."

"No, on the contrary. Having to talk about her past can be a good thing. It helps with her cognitive flow and memory. She just got flustered that those memories of hers weren't cooperating."

"Can I see her?"

"I would suggest letting her get some rest for now. Why don't you go and get yourself something to eat from the coffee shop around the corner? They have a great Friday special on a coffee and doughnut combo today. It will do you good to get some fresh air."

"Thank you for being so kind to me, Tracy."

"Well, I appreciate you spending time with Sarah. She isn't the friendliest person to be around, but everyone deserves love and kindness, no matter how bad you want to kick them!"

The two women laughed, helping to put Mia's mind at ease. She wanted to ask Tracy more about Sarah and her condition, but she figured she'd worn everyone out for the time being with her questions.

The walk calmed her. There was something about the crisp autumn breeze and its fresh, welcoming scent that made Mia feel at peace. The friendly passersby greeted her with smiles and simple nods. Her steps felt airy and light, as if they were her first. She admired the clean sidewalks and peaceful scenery. Life seemed to move by gradually, unhurried and patient. She'd been with Sarah for only a short time, yet it seemed as though she'd been there a lifetime. Each sip of her warm hazelnut coffee sent a warm sensation through her, and she kept her leisurely pace until she was once again standing in the nursing home's pristine yard.

Mia ran her eyes across the pathways and porch, hoping to catch a glimpse of Tracy or Sarah. She finally spotted the two women out by a shaded sitting area. Tracy sat on a rusty steel garden bench, Sarah nestled in her wheelchair nearby. Mia walked over to them, quietly so as not to interrupt Tracy reading to Sarah. Tracy looked up from the pages of the thick novel and smiled at Mia.

“Did you enjoy your walk?”

“It was great. Got my mind off things. I feel much better now.” Mia looked down at Sarah, whose chin was drooping onto her chest. She looked as if she were fast asleep. Tracy folded a corner of the page, closing the book. She held her hand up towards her mouth, keeping her words quiet.

“I’ve been reading to her for a little while,” she whispered. “She may be out of it right now. We gave her some medicine this morning. She may not remember too much about what happened, so keep the conversation light for now. You’re welcome to sit down and continue if you would like.”

“That’s fine with me.” Mia took the book from Tracy, and the two switched positions. Tracy left Mia and Sarah alone, heading off to tend to the other residents. Mia cracked open the book, where Tracy had left off and began to read the worn pages of *A Tale of Two Cities*.

“Making his way through the tainted crowd—”

“Where the hell have you been?” Mia looked up from her book to see Sarah staring directly at her. Sarah’s eyes had a dull, pinkish hue, and her wrinkled face was twisted into a frown of displeasure.

“Sadie! You’re awake!” Mia cheered with excitement.

“I’ve been awake. I play dead sometimes. It keeps Tracy off my back.”

“I’m sorry I stepped out for a little while to get some coffee. I didn’t think you would mind.”

“Well, I do mind. You get me used to your company, and then you leave without telling me. Shame on you!”

“I’m here now,” Mia said, placing her hand on Sarah’s knee. “Do you want me to continue reading?”

“Yeah, yeah. Go on. I don’t want to go back inside right now. It’s too nice out here.”

Mia returned to the pages of the book and continued reading to Sarah.

A few chapters later, Mia heard the clanging of a bell off in the distance.

"It's lunchtime, child. Wheel me in. I'm hungry."

"Yes, ma'am." Mia placed the book under her arm and began pushing Sarah back into the building. The cafeteria was empty at that moment, giving Mia the opportunity to wheel Sarah to the best seat in the room, right beside the fruit table.

"You know what I like. I'll be right here," Sarah huffed. Mia again wandered through the cafeteria, grabbing a few items she knew would make Sarah happy. She returned to the table and set them before her.

"What did you get?" Sarah said, looking over at Mia's tray.

"I got a sandwich and chips." Mia popped open her bag of potato chips and began crunching away. Sarah pushed the food that Mia had placed in front of her to the side and leaned back in her wheelchair, folding her arms. The displeased frown was back.

"Tell me the truth. Why did you leave? They have coffee right here in this cafeteria. Why did you leave?"

Mia looked up, puzzled. She wasn't sure if Sarah had forgotten what had happened, but she didn't want to cause her to become upset again.

"I promise, I went to get coffee. That's all."

"Well, I'm getting used to you being here now. Talking to you is nice. Next time you are going to leave, you can at least say goodbye. Don't be rude."

"Yes, ma'am." Mia went back to eating her chips. She wasn't sure how to change the subject and start a new conversation with Sarah. She was nervous to say anything about Lucinda or anything to do with her past again. It was clearly a heavy topic to talk about. She decided to change the subject, thinking it would help and not harm.

"What do you have planned to do today?" Mia asked, hoping to get started on the right foot. Sarah looked at Mia with confusion.

"I thought we were talking about something before you left. What were we talking about?" Mia froze and looked away from Sarah, trying to find something else to discuss.

"We were talking about your late husband's paintings on the wall, remember."

"No, I wasn't talking about those. I was talking about something else. I told you something else. What was it?" Mia saw Sarah growing confused, so she blurted out the truth.

"Lucinda. You were telling me about Lucinda."

Sarah paused for a few moments and looked down at her hands. They were shaking. She had taken her medication. Seeing her hands move without her permission brought back the morning's events.

"I remember now. I'm sorry you saw me that way. I get confused sometimes. I've lost a lot of my memories, but the thought of losing her would kill me. That time with her is sacred to me. She taught me so much."

Mia reached out and grabbed Sarah's hands. "You don't have to apologize to me. I love you just the way you are. You don't have to talk about her anymore. I can see how much you care for her."

"I did. Still do. I know I was only with her for a few days, but she meant a lot to me. Felt like I was talking to my momma again, being with someone who was strict but cared about me. There's no greater feeling in this world than to be loved that way. I felt like I was with family. I never did get to know my grandmothers. They were both dead and gone before I got a chance to know who they were. Momma never talked much about them or any of our family except her brother. On the rare occasions when she did bring up her mother, she'd always say how quiet and distant she was. There wasn't much more to speak on than that."

"I don't have much of a family either," Mia said.

"You have your mother, don't you?"

"I don't consider her *family*."

"Whether you like it or not, she's your family," Sarah nudged Mia's arm. "I heard you in the hallway earlier. I heard the way you spoke to your mother. You should forgive her. Let go of that hurt."

"I don't know if I will ever be able to forgive her. She's the reason I never knew you. She's the reason for my loneliness. I don't want to ruin our time together talking about her. I'm happy here with you."

"Well, you'll get a pass for now. I'm your family now, too. I hope that suits you."

"That suits me just fine!" said Mia.

"I'm feeling a little better now. So, hush up, child, and let me try and finish my story!"

CHAPTER TWENTY-THREE

BREAKDOWN

"I carried my paper and pen with me each day. I hoped she'd give me words to fill the pages, but each day I returned with nothing more than dirty hands and messy hair. It became routine for me to get to her door, hear her instructions, and get to work with an unwavering 'yes, ma'am.' I wanted to give up every day, but there was something drawing me back to that dilapidated cabin, something I couldn't explain. My mind was telling me I didn't have to do what I was doing, but my heart told me she needed my help and that's where I belonged. Each day, I would come in, eager to know if that would be the day she'd open up and talk to me about her past.

"She began to speak to me while I worked. I guess after she revealed what was under her head wrap, she felt more inclined to trust me with conversation. It was nothing deep at first. She started with simple questions, like 'Where ya from?' and 'Ya know how tuh cook?' I would give her short responses, never going into much detail, afraid she'd stop talking to me if I said too much. She kept her eyes on me while I worked. Watching me sweat like a man and messing up my clean clothes.

"I remember one day I was dusting those old books piled up in the corner. I must've turned too quickly because I accidentally knocked over

the whole pile. They all toppled over and made a loud thud on the old floorboards. Lucinda was outside at the time, feeding Ol' Ben. She rushed inside to see what had happened and found me trying to pick them up one by one. She came over to me and snatched one of the books out of my hand, scolding me for being so careless.

"'Ya got no respect? Dem books older den me! Dey my dear Mary's books, an' I won't have 'em harmed all 'cause ah some clumsy gal!'

"I apologized for my carelessness and continued picking up the books from the floor. I watched her from the corner of my eye as she dusted off the book she was holding in her hand, running her fingers along the raised words on the cover and sighing to herself. I wanted to ask her why the books were so important to her. They were old and covered in dust. She placed the book down and spoke to me as if she heard my thoughts.

"'I ain't know much when she find me. Slaves ain't allowed tuh even hold books, much less open ah cover an' take peak inside. I's just like any slave she seen come an' go, but God seen fit tuh put us together. She teach me everythin' I know. My words all broken an' small 'fore I met her. Dey still broken but dey done got big. I know big words like 'eloquent' an' 'underestimated.' Still got much I don't know. I stop tryin' tuh read dem pages when she left dis good Earth. I let dat dust have its way now.'

"I could see she slipped into deep thought about this woman named Mary. I stood there and let her speak. She finally snapped out of it and walked over to grab my arm.

"'Take care of dem books, gal. I ain't gonna say it again.'

"I stayed out of her way after that, careful not to upset her again. She still stayed close. Watching me work, watching me sweat. She stayed quiet too, until later that day, when I was down on the floor fixing a lifted floorboard, she stood up from her chair and walked over to me.

"'I been watchin' ya an' waitin' on ya tuh get tired an' leave me be. Must be God who sent ya here. All dem others dat come tuh my door,

got ah look on 'em. I can't put my finger on it. Dey just look like dey not right. But ya look like ya sent here. I wanna trust ya. I got ah feelin' in me ya ain't gonna judge me for what I done. 'Fore I say my peace, I got tuh know ya better. Dem eyes say ya been through things. What ya been through, gal?'

"She gave me a moment, then she asked me again. I had no reason to keep anything from her. I felt as though she already knew the truth. She wanted to see if I was going to be honest. I broke down and told her everything. How I needed money to support myself. How my momma had just passed away, and I hadn't been able to find much work. How I was sorry for not caring about getting her story at first because all I needed was the money. I started crying, watching my tears form a puddle on the broken floorboard.

"She told me to get up. She walked us back over to the chair so she could sit down. I sat on the floor next to her. She handed me a piece of cloth from her apron to wipe my face and tapped her leg, telling me to lay my head on her thigh. I felt like she could finally see me. I could feel she wanted to trust me. I know she wasn't mean. She was hurt by the past. It did what it has done to me too. Makes you want to be alone because being alone keeps you safe. It keeps you guarded from the pain that loving people can bring.

"My tears started to flow even harder. I continued on, telling her about Momma being sick and Poppa dying in the war. I told her about how I gave up after Momma died and that I didn't care about much anymore. I told her about my normal, boring life washing clothes and wanting to become a teacher. I told her about the nights I cried. I even blurted things I didn't even know were ailing me. Like being alone, without family or anyone to love. I told her that I never knew anyone from my family and that I never looked at all the pictures that my momma kept in boxes because I was too scared to see their faces. Faces of people who

I could never love. Faces of people who were dead and gone. No life to be found in any of them.

"I let my tears and all the things that were on my mind get soaked up into her tattered old dress. I felt something for her at that moment. Something I will never be able to explain. I know she felt it, too. She kept stroking my hair and letting me cry, not saying a word until I couldn't say anything else. All the words poured out of me. I was exhausted, as if I'd just run a race. I wiped my face dry. I knew I said too much. I pressed my hands into the floor and tried to lift myself to get back to working on the floorboard. She pushed my shoulder back, telling me to stay put. I remember her looking me in my eyes as her deep voice tried to calm me.

"'I know what it be like watchin' someone die in front of yo' eyes. Someone ya love. I don't talk much after everythin' I seen. Just keep tuh myself. Not gonna be here on dis good Earth much longer. Used tuh pray for someone I could tell what I been through. Clear my conscience an' get right with God 'fore I die, cuz I done things I ain't proud of. Den here ya come. Tuh listen an' hear what I got tuh say. Had tuh make sure ya duh right one. I's made up my mind. Gonna give ya what ya come for. Don't much care who finds out. I ain't got duh strength tuh run. Truth got tuh be told. Promise me ya gone tell 'em just what I say. Don't leave out nothin', got dat? Well, go an' get dat paper ya got. I's ready now."

CHAPTER TWENTY-FOUR

REWARDED

"I want to go back to my room now." Sarah pulled her shawl tightly around her arms. The air in the cafeteria was chilly, and Mia could see a look of discomfort on Sarah's face.

"Are you feeling okay?"

"I don't like the cold air. Hurts to move." Mia cleared the table and quickly wheeled Sarah out of the cafeteria.

"She was the one who got me writing, you know," Sarah muttered as Mia pushed her down the empty hallway. "She stirred up something in me I never knew was there."

"Are you feeling up to telling me more of her story, Sadie?"

"I don't have a choice. I've been hurting for a long time because of what I chose to do. I had my reasons. I thought I was doing more good than harm. My selfishness did me and Lucinda an injustice. You're going to hear her story, but from her, not from me."

Once inside the room, Sarah pointed to the closet by the door. "Go in there and bring that tote back over here. You didn't dig deep enough last time."

Mia rushed over to the closet and again dragged the heavy tote back to the kitchen table. Sarah instructed Mia to dig to the bottom. She rummaged around for a few moments, and finally, another shoebox came into view. It, too, was covered in red twine.

“Open it,” Sarah instructed.

Mia grabbed the scissors from the table, slipping her fingers into the cold metal holes once more. She began cutting away the twine until it all fell in a pile around her. She opened the box to find several sheets of folded, yellowed paper inside. Mia could see the pages were old and stained with water and oil smudges.

“I may lose my memories of her,” Sarah whispered, “but I will always have her words close by.”

“What are these?” Mia asked, carefully lifting the corners of the pages in the box to see how many there were.

“After all my days of doing chores for her and sweating like a man, she finally decided to tell me her story. Every precious memory of hers is right there.”

“There are a lot of pages here.”

“She had a lot to say. She was probably close to a hundred years old when I met her. She was never sure of her actual age. She had decades of memories piled up. She only got to tell me a snippet of it all. I couldn’t begin to tell you every word now. My memories of that time are fading.”

“So, this is her story. It’s all here! That’s amazing!” Mia said.

“It took some time for her to get everything out, but there it is. I wrote it all down first, then went back and typed it all out on those very pages. I sat on the floor right beside her while she stared up at the ceiling. She kept her eyes closed the entire time. I didn’t interrupt. I just wrote every word she said. Go ahead, start from the beginning. Read it out loud. I want to get close to her again.”

Mia reached to pull out the papers, but remembered how to care for fragile artifacts. She decided to get a pair of latex gloves to handle the delicate pieces of paper first. She found a discarded pair by the kitchen sink. Mia carefully lifted the first page from the box. The paper had faded, and the black typewriter ink had worn away, causing some words to bleed into one another. Luckily, time hadn't caused too much damage to the pages. Mia took a deep breath and began.

CHAPTER TWENTY-FIVE

LUCINDA

"I don't know my name. Yes, duh name I's given be Lucinda, but I don't know my name. Don't know who I's supposed tuh be 'fore I be Lucinda. 'Fore I be someone's slave. I imagine what dat sweet name coulda been. Dat name my mama give tuh me. I don't know who I's supposed tuh be, but I know who I be now. I's give what I can from duh memories of mine dat ain't dried up an' withered away. I's start with duh first day dat I 'member, 'cause no other days matter 'fore dat.

"Duh heat. I 'member duh heat. Dat air thick an' stale. I 'member duh rock I's standin' on hot as duh air dat choked my lungs. My feet small. Dey burnt an' blackened by duh sun. Dere be folk everywhere. I 'member dem pale, white people, covered in fine linens an' suits. I 'member lookin' down at my little naked body, exposed for all dem pale, white people tuh gawk at. Duh skin on duh soles of my feet burnin'. I 'member hoppin' back an' forth, tryin' tuh let duh pain go away in one foot 'fore pressin' it back down on duh scoldin' hot rock. Duh white folk laughed an' enjoyed my childish dance. Dey dumb tuh my pain. My pain pleased 'em.

"I felt duh chain round my neck pull. She standin' dere, lookin' down at me. Still can see her clear as day. Still see her deep brown eyes full of places I ain't never seen. Dat thick black hair platted 'round her head like ah' crown. Her beautiful black skin shined with lines of cool sweat. Still can see her smile. All dat made me fret, gone away. All 'cause I see her smile. But I see her smile gone away. She looked 'round confused 'cause ah man come tuh unchain me. Her face lost dat beautiful smile. Her smile turn twisted an' screams come pourin' out her mouth. Duh man grabbed her up an' muttered somethin'. He looked down at me an' shook his head. He patted me on my head an' turned away, talkin' tuh other pale people in duh crowd. She grabbed me an' pulled me close. Her heart racin'. Her arms shakin'. She start whisperin' in my ear. Whisperin' words I don't know. "Nitakupata! Nitakupata!" I still hear her clear as day. She repeatin' it over an' over.

"Den I seen her reachin' for somethin'. Only took ah' second, with duh man's back turned an' duh crowd lookin' away. She grabbed my leg an' dug ah' sharp piece of metal in it. Dug duh metal deep in my leg an' pressed her hand over my mouth. I screamed in pain 'tween her wet fingers. Duh moment gone an' dere on my leg be ah' bloody mark. She marked me. Duh man turned 'round, slappin' her, hard. He an' other men pulled her away from me. She screamin' an' cryin'. Duh man poured hot whiskey on my leg an' wrapped cloth 'round my bloody mark. I still hear her screams from duh crowd. Mine just as loud. My little eyes searched for her. Dat's duh last time I seen her face. Dat's duh day I lost my mama.

"Now dat I's able tuh understand duh world, I know I's sold off dat day. Torn from duh arms of my mama an' inta hell. I become duh property of ah' man name Massa Gavin. He ah' young man, tall an' slender with ah' head full ah' fire red hair. Dat's how I know he duh devil. After returnin' home from schoolin' up in Boston, he come tuh find his folks dead from ah' outbreak of typhoid. Cleared out half duh plantation. He made tuh continue duh horrible trade of slave breedin' his father passed down. After clearin' out duh dead an' gettin' dat big plantation back tuh normal, Massa Gavin down tuh only ah' few good ones. He got tuh purchasin' more slave gals, an' I's ah' part of his breedin' collection. Ain't matter dat blood ain't start tuh fall from 'tween my legs. I come tuh him cheap an' ripe for labor 'round duh plantation.

"Massa Gavin got me an' two other gals dat day. One named Bella an' duh other Mattie. He give us tuh duh other slaves on duh plantation. Dey give us full understandin' of what we doin' once we come of age. We tuh work as hard as any other gal on dat plantation. All us worked, pregnant or not.

"By day, we made tuh tend tuh duh plantation. We wash clothes, seed an' pull harvest in duh small fields 'round duh plantation. Dere always somethin' tuh be done. By night, duh gals on ah' strict schedule. Those who won't with child taken tuh shacks in duh corner of duh field, an' made tuh wait 'til duh bucks arrived. Bucks not allowed tuh stay pass mornin' on Massa Gavin's plantation. His father made it so an' Massa Gavin keep tuh dat rule. Big, strong black negro men brought in at night from ah neighborin' plantation. He found it best tuh bring in duh bucks. Dat way he ain't got tuh deal with ownin', handlin' an' keepin' watch over 'em. He say his gals tuh be untouched 'til he say so. He meant dat.

"Massa Gavin got lots of slave gals come an' go from duh plantation. Some sold after not producin' chillun. Some died while givin' birth. We all tuh breed other slaves, tuh be sold or live on duh plantation tuh continue duh cycle. Massa

Gavin got ah' strict schedule of breedin' tuh uphold. Each season dat come, new babies be born. If we did anythin' tuh mess up dat schedule, like losin' ah baby while it still in us, we got lashes from dat cowhide whip. Not much time 'tween babies if we did birth one. Massa Gavin ain't give us no time tuh get back on our feet 'fore we got another buck on top of us. He say dat nigger gals built for breedin' babies. He say it be God's will. Massa Gavin ah' cruel man, indeed.

"Massa Gavin got ah wife. Her name Martha. She just as cruel as him. Not sure who be worse at times, him or her. Maybe somewhere in her heart she kind, but we never seen it. She never smiled or find one kind word for us. She cold an' callous. Martha birth six chillun by duh time we come tuh duh plantation. Maybe she always mean cuz Massa Gavin keep puttin' babies in her, knowin' she sick. She plagued by duh loss of her hair, an' no doctor Virginia able tuh cure her. I 'member seein' her in duh windows of duh big house in duh mornin', without her wig. She looked like ah walkin' skeleton, an' scared me every time. Martha ain't allow us tuh walk 'round wit' heads full of thick hair. She seen our hair as mockery. As if duh strands laughin' at her. She hated us for it. So, she shaved us bald so dat we ain't upset her. We keep our heads shaved clean or else we got whipped. Massa Gavin never put ah stop tuh it. Long as we able tuh breed, he ain't care 'bout anythin' else. Duh day me, Bella an' Mattie get tuh duh plantation, dere be ah pair of shiny scissors waitin' for all us."

CHAPTER TWENTY-SIX

CRAWL

Mia stopped.

She placed the yellowed pages down on the table. She had so many questions she wanted to ask Sarah. So many things she wanted to say. She was speechless.

"You okay, child?" Sarah asked.

"I don't know what to say right now. This is a lot to unpack."

"You! Speechless? Can't be! You've got questions for your questions! Go on, ask me something. I know it's coming."

Mia hung her head. "I don't want to ask a dumb question or say anything stupid. I tend to do that a lot. I'll keep reading."

"What makes you feel that way?" Sarah reached out and tapped Mia on the hand.

"I don't know much about slavery other than what I was taught in school or what Lucinda went through. I don't know what it's like to be *black* or have it mean something to me. It makes me feel awkward and stupid just thinking about it."

"You're not stupid, child. A little ditzy, maybe, but certainly not stupid. I didn't know much about all of this at first, either. Slavery and all the pain that came with it were foreign concepts to me. So much of our past has faded away like leaves on a tree. Blossoming one moment and dead in the dirt the next. There are things we will never know because time has taken them away, but we should learn what we can while we can. You have to learn to crawl before you can walk. I learned to crawl, then walk and then run! So you have to read and crawl first, child. Read and crawl!"

Mia smiled at Sarah. "I do have a question for you, Sadie."

"Well, spit it out already!"

"Did Lucinda ever show you her scar?" Sarah looked at Mia, trying to remember if there was an answer to her question. She paused for a few moments. Then it came to her.

"She did," she replied, "she showed it to me. It was hiding there in the folds of her wrinkled skin. It was very hard to see. I couldn't make out what it was supposed to be at first. But then I saw it was a long line with an X at the bottom, sort of like a treasure map. I remember I was so curious that I reached out to touch it. I thought she was going to slap me for being so forward. To my surprise, she said nothing. It felt like a message written in Braille. It had these small bumps and grooves under it." Sarah began feeling her own wrinkled skin, mimicking the moment.

"And her hair…I can't believe someone would be so cruel as to cut a child's hair off like that. It makes no sense."

"A lot of cruel things happen every day, child. We have no choice but to keep going. Lucinda's hair never grew back from all the times she was shaved and cut. I understood right then and there why she felt the way she did about my hair, and you better understand why I feel the same way about yours."

"Yes, ma'am, I do." Mia sighed. She picked up the papers to begin again, but was interrupted by a knock at the door. Tracy poked her head through the door and signaled to Mia to come meet her out in the hallway.

"How are things going with Sarah?" Tracy whispered.

"They're going great! I'm getting a little hungry, so we will probably be wrapping up soon and going to dinner." Mia felt her stomach growl.

"I can bring dinner in for you both a little later. I have to make sure Sarah takes her medication before bed. We don't want any more incidents with her that can be prevented."

"Okay. No problem."

"One other thing," Tracy continued. "Has she asked about her TV soaps yet?"

"No, she hasn't said anything to me about that."

"Well, I promise you, she will soon. Sarah's a die-hard *Days of Our Lives* fan. She never misses an episode, but she's missed a few since you got here. I'm pretty sure at some point she's going to remember and want to watch them. I wanted to let you know, just in case she has an outburst. Don't worry, though; I record all the soap operas for the residents just in case they miss one or fall asleep during the show. If she asks, just take her into the recreation room. The tapes are on top of the TV."

"Tracy, I don't know what we would do without you." Mia sighed.

"No need to thank me! I appreciate you keeping her company." Tracy smiled and made her way back down the dimly lit hallway.

Mia slipped back inside the room and closed the door. She sat back in her seat at the table and gave Sarah a loving smile.

"Now, where were we?" Mia asked.

"What did Tracy want?"

"Just wanted to check on you and see about dinner, that's all."

"Well, you can go on and keep reading for now. Dinner isn't ready yet," Sarah huffed. "Lucinda's got plenty more to say."

CHAPTER TWENTY-SEVEN

LITTLE ONE

"Don't recall much growin' up. Days just blend together now, but duh summer I become ah' woman still clear. First, I got tuh speak 'bout Bess. Good ol' Bess. She duh one Massa Gavin give me tuh when I got tuh duh plantation. Bess ah' small, stout woman, but her presence command respect. Even Massa Gavin an' Martha lax when it come tuh Bess. Bess even got tuh keep her hair, but she wrapped it up good an' never let Martha see. Bess good 'bout not pushin' her luck.

Bess duh head of duh big house. She duh only one of us dat never did breed. She well on in years but still 'round tuh tend tuh Martha's needs an' help raise chillun. She raised many gals like me, an' seen 'em come an' go. Bess teach me everythin' I know. She duh one dat tell me 'bout Massa Gavin an' what happened 'fore I got dere. She one of duh lucky ones dat ain't catch duh typhoid. She teach me how tuh cook, clean an' be ah good servant. She strict with me but I's lucky tuh get her even if she ain't show me much love.

"Me an' Bess outside workin' on Martha's laundry one day. I 'member she looked down at my dress at duh blood stained in duh cloth. I ain't even notice. Swore it be sweat drippin' from me. She grabbed me up an' hugged me tight. First time she ever did hug me. She whispered in my ear dat it be time an' pushed me away. She wiped tears from her eyes an' called Massa Gavin tuh come see. He come bouncin' down tuh where we at with ah' big ol' smile on his face. Took one look at my dress an' clapped his hands, excited. Bess took my hand an' led me tuh one of duh gals who good at breedin'. Her name Leah. Leah be Massa Gavin's best gal. She birthed only boys an' pregnant again. Boys made Massa duh most money. Massa love Leah. He always rubbin' on her shoulder or lookin' her in her eyes like he love her. She beautiful, with skin duh color of warm peaches an' curvy hips. She bald as any of duh rest of us an' still beautiful. Massa Gavin's rule of no touchin' his gals meant he ain't allowed either. If things different, I's sure he been had his way with her.

"Leah took me from Bess an' showed me 'round duh cabins. I ain't never been in duh cabins, but played near 'em from time tuh time. Won't nothin' in 'em but ah straw bed an' some candles. She show me what tuh do an' how tuh make sure I do things right duh first time. She tell me tuh stay on top of 'em, cuz duh men be so tired from workin' all day dat dey fall asleep right on top ah' us! Leah say one of 'em almost killed her cuz he so heavy! She good tuh me an' teach me everythin' I needed tuh know. An' so my life as ah breedin' slave started.

"Things ain't start off good for me. I's one of duh troubled women on duh plantation. Dat's what Massa Gavin say. I ain't think dat I's troubled, just dat my babies smart tuh what life dey comin' in tuh an' chose death right dere in my belly. My babies ain't stay put. Few summers went by, an' I lost six babies. I buried 'em in duh woods outside duh plantation. Chose ah spot next tuh ah' stream where dey be safe. I stopped cryin' after duh first one. I started tuh rejoice dat dey safe with God an' away from dat place. Massa Gavin beat me hard each time my babies died. Duh skin from my back be duh price I paid for allowin' "his property" tuh die. I never understood it, but he say it be my fault. Bess an' duh others always cleanin' my back an' gettin' me back tuh good health. Massa Gavin say duh next time my baby die, he gonna do away with me. He vowed tuh hitch me tuh his cart an' drag me off tuh town tuh be sold. He meant dat.

"One day God spared my back ah lashin', an' ah baby come outta me on ah cold winter night. Tall buck named Paul be duh one dat make it happen. He give me ah little baby gal. She be duh tiniest thing I ever seen. Her skin dark an' deep like ah hot summer night. She bald as her backside, so I's happy for dat at least. She looked up at me with blood an' water all over her face. Her warm breath made little clouds of white smoke in duh freezin' air. She seen me an' I seen her. One of duh women asked me what I's gonna name her. I laughed. Why waste time with givin' her ah name? I's sure Massa Gavin gonna take her from me soon. I's numb by dat time. But dere be somethin' in her eyes dat called tuh me, wantin' me tuh love her. Next mornin', Massa Gavin come an' grabbed my baby right out my arms. He inspected her with ah smile. Told me things lookin' up for me. He say I better take good care of dis one an' not kill her like I killed duh others. If I did, he sure tuh hang me. He meant dat. He handed her back tuh me an' walked off, but not 'fore tellin' me tuh raise her up right 'til he ready tuh sell her. I begged for him tuh let her stay. He laughed an' say he dare not keep ah baby dat come from me. I's already ah bigger burden den he want. If he keep her, she sure tuh kill her babies, like me.

"Massa Gavin right 'bout one thing. Things started tuh look up for me for once. He normally come an' take babies off tuh auction when dey start walkin'. Dem boys be duh ones he got duh best price for, cuz everyone in town see duh hard-workin' bucks dey come from. Massa Gavin auction 'em off with duh promise dat dey able tuh be molded an' taught tuh obey from ah young age. Dat's what makes ah good slave. Dey valuable 'cause not one seen or heard duh fairy-tale called freedom. But my baby ah gal. Ah already cursed gal dat he wanted no parts of.

"So, I hid her. Hid her good. Hid her on my back, under wraps while washin' clothes. When duh spring come, I hid her in tall grass out in duh field. Even hid her under my body while we slept. Bess say she be duh best baby she ever seen. My baby never fuss or cry. She ah happy, quiet baby. She come outta me at duh best time. Massa forgot 'bout her at one point. Leah an' Mattie both birth twin boys in duh same week. Massa Gavin all excited with such ah profit. My baby gal duh last thing on his mind. Massa Gavin called us all in front of duh big house one day an' say he headin' tuh Norfolk tuh fetch ah buyer for duh boys. Dat's duh first time he left us with Martha, but it won't duh last. Don't 'member how long Massa Gavin gone but 'member my baby gal talkin' small words when Massa Gavin finally come home.

"Massa Gavin upset when he showed back up. He say dat no more bucks comin' 'round for ah while. He say ain't no buyers either tuh take duh boys. His neighbor an' partner skipped town with all his bucks. Some man name Lincoln messin' everythin' up for Massa Gavin. He cursed an' spit on his name all duh time. We tuh continue doin' our daily chores an' tendin' tuh duh plantation 'til Massa get more bucks. Losin' 'em bucks like watchin' money float away down ah river. Bess say Massa Gavin need money tuh keep duh plantation goin'.

"I ain't never seen or felt freedom 'fore dat time, but it started tuh feel like I's free. Massa Gavin started leavin' duh plantation more an' more. He gone most of duh day an' come home smelly an' drunk at night. Massa Gavin turn tuh duh bottle after losin' 'em bucks an' we all seen it. Martha left alone with us durin' duh day. She never spoke tuh us 'bout anythin' else but work. We tended tuh her needs an' took care of her rotten, spoiled chillun. She ain't no overseer. She slept most of duh time an' refused tuh come outside. Massa Gavin never got ah overseer. No one dere tuh keep us from runnin'. Ain't hard tuh find ah bald slave woman runnin' away. Dere be nowhere safer than dat plantation. No fences or walls tuh keep us from escapin', but we stayed put. It be duh fear of duh outside dat keep us still. Knowin' what patty rollers do tuh us or even worse, what ah Massa who thirst for black gals do tuh us.

"While Martha slept an' 'em rotten chillun ran free, we sang an' tended tuh work. My baby gal stayed right by my side. She drank me dry an' got chunky, with thick little legs an' skin duh color of pine tree bark. Her eyes deep an' lovin'. I 'member when she start tuh crawl, den walk, an' den run. I never give her ah real name while she with me. Her name Little One. She smiled an' danced with me an' duh other gals. It felt good. Her little mouth spilled out broken words like mine, but I still know exactly what she be needin'. I know when she needed water an' when she needed food. Bess carried her tuh duh kitchen almost every day tuh help her cook. She played with Leah an' Mattie's boys an' chased 'em all 'round duh fields. She got smarter an' more beautiful every day. Every day I loved her ah little more. Every day

I grew more dumb tuh her fate. My Little One not ah slave in my eyes, but ah child whose hands clean an' soft with no signs of labor. Our misguided freedom went on 'til Spring come 'round again. No one beat. No one sold. We watched duh days an' nights come an' go, with no idea what gonna happen.

"'Bout duh time Spring be comin' 'round again, be when Bess come tuh all us sayin' she hear ah conversation. Martha in duh parlor, speakin' tuh ah neighbor friend 'bout duh problem with Massa Gavin. She say Massa Gavin losin' money. He pilferin' away all dey done earned an' saved. Everythin' his father done worked so hard for goin' tuh drinkin' an' gamblin'. She say he done lost his mind frettin' over some war. Devil done got hold of her husband an' she desperate tuh help him. She frettin' like Massa Gavin 'cause she ain't sure how much longer things gonna be duh same. Bess come an' tell us what she know, but we ain't know what tuh make of it.

Dere been talk amongst duh others 'bout war goin' on. Duh bucks dat once come tuh lay on top of us an' whispered rumors in our ears. Dey tell stories dat white people wanna fight for us tuh be free. Massa Gavin never say nothin' 'bout it tuh us. So we thinkin' it be all talk an' no truth tuh it. We hear gunshots an' loud bangs sometimes, but Massa Gavin always say some excuse 'bout what duh noise be. Sometimes it be ah runaway slave gettin' caught by patty rollers. Sometimes he say dey levelin' duh ground for ah new plantation. Anythin' tuh keep us dumb an' from gettin' any ideas in our heads. We thought it safe tuh say dat if dere indeed be ah war goin' on, dat it be white people who fightin' an' slaves got nothin' tuh do with it.

"After she finish tellin' us everythin' she heard, she let duh others go, an' pulled me 'round back of duh big house tuh finish her news. Bess got ah sad look in her eyes. Never gonna forget dat look. She tell me duh lady friend dat Martha speakin' tuh got ah daughter. She be wantin' her tuh have her own slave gal tuh play with. My Little One duh only baby gal on duh plantation an' she offered up for ah nice price. Martha needed duh money. Bess say Massa Gavin gotta say yes first, but she sure dey gonna take her. All duh happiness I felt drained from me. All duh joy in my heart, gone.

"Dat night, I paced ah hole in dat cabin floor. We slept peacefully for so many nights. Dere ain't nothin' I coulda done tuh stop 'em from takin' her. I know what be comin'. I know if ever I did find her, dat I need tuh know who she be an' dat she mine. I's unsure what tuh do, 'til I looked down at my leg an' seen duh mark my mama put on me. I's never sure why she done it. I always believed she gone mad. But, I felt her right in dat moment. I swear she start talkin' tuh me. Tellin' me dat she mark me so dat she able tuh find me, an' now I needed tuh do duh same tuh my Little One. One day, she promised, duh mark gonna bring us back together.

"I ain't fret after dat. I'member how frantic my mama been when she carved duh mark in my leg. No need. Some moonlight still left tuh do what needed tuh be done. Massa Gavin left ah bottle ah whiskey down by duh water basin. I snuck out duh cabin an' grabbed dat bottle an' pulled some linen off duh line. I grabbed my Little One in my arms an' looked deep in dem eyes. I say exactly what come tuh me. I say, "You got ah name. Your name Nitakupata. 'Member yo' name, 'cause it belongs tuh us both." I tried my best tuh make it painless for her. It be duh only way I know I's able tuh 'member her if I ever found her again. She still filled with sleep, unsure of what I's sayin' or why I's cryin'. She whispered "Momma" tuh me when I poured duh warm whiskey down her throat. I watched her get all dizzy an' finally pass out. Her little faint cries still rang out when I started cravin' duh same mark in her my mama carved in me. I wrapped her little leg up an' held her tight. I drank what be left in duh bottle tuh help me sleep an' drown out her pain. Don't 'member how long we slept an' don't 'member duh sun comin' up dat mornin'. I 'member when I woke up, she gone."

CHAPTER TWENTY-EIGHT

BURDENED

Lucinda's words were heavy.

Sarah shifted from eager to despondent while Mia read from the yellowed pages. Mia could see that Sarah was doing her best to hide her sadness. Lucinda's pain was tangible. It was hard and dense, impossible to swallow. Tracy had quietly slipped into the room while Mia was reading and delivered dinner. The air instantly filled with the aroma of Salisbury steak and steamed vegetables. Mia felt her stomach contest any further delay, and the two women ate in silence.

Afterwards, Mia and Sarah both agreed they'd read enough for one day. Mia assisted Sarah to her bedroom so she could retire for the evening. She found a comfortable spot in the couch's creases and spent most of the night checking her phone and texting Bee about her day until she drifted off to sleep.

As the morning sun crept into the window, the sharp rays of light pierced Mia's eyes. Her tired body lay sprawled on the couch, with limbs pointing in every direction. She flipped the lumpy pillow over to shield her face and continued to snore into the air.

A heavy slap on her shoulder startled her. She came to, rolling her body around, unsure of who or what had hit her. There was Sarah, hovering over her, looking more irritated than usual in her wheelchair.

"You made me miss my stories! It's Saturday, and I missed my stories! How am I supposed to know what Marlena and John are doing if I don't watch my stories?!"

Mia rubbed her face and sat up, still groggy and in need of rest. To anyone else, the abrupt slap and rude awakening would've triggered an argument, but Mia had more patience and love for Sarah than anyone. She knew patience and love were what Sarah needed the most.

"You didn't miss them, Sadie. Tracy recorded all of your stories for you. We can go to the rec room so you can watch them."

"Well, what are we waiting for? Let's go!"

Mia, still groggy and tired, only wanted to see Sarah happy. She wiped the stale drool from the corners of her mouth and got to work pushing Sarah's wheelchair down the creaking floorboards of the hallway. Once inside the recreation room, Mia was surprised to find several other residents up early, gathered around a large TV. Everyone was quiet and focused on the people moving around on the screen. Mia pushed Sarah to an empty section of the room and locked her wheelchair in place. Mia looked around the large room, which was covered with large bookshelves and stacks of board games. She was relieved to find Tracy reading a magazine in the corner. She waved at Mia and walked over to her.

"You look exhausted. Is the couch not working out for you anymore?"

"No, the couch is fine," Mia groaned. "I didn't get much sleep last night. We did a lot of reading yesterday, and it drained me, that's all."

"Well, I'm going to need you to go back in there and get some more rest. You look like hell!"

“She wants to watch her stories. Is that what everyone else is watching right now?”

“They’re finishing up Good Morning America right now. We can start Days of Our Lives in a few minutes. You go back in the room and get some rest. I’ll make sure she gets some breakfast and gets up to speed about Marlena.”

“Thank you, Tracy.” Mia smiled and retreated to the room. She spread herself back on the couch and fell into a deep, peaceful sleep.

Mia woke up feeling refreshed. She peered around the room, now void of Sarah’s magnetic presence. Without her, the room became lifeless and dull. A room without Sarah was a reality Mia never wanted to experience. Mia brushed away the somber thought. She’d slept past lunchtime and needed to get back to Sarah. She headed into Sarah’s room to take a shower, abruptly stopping in the doorway, remembering Sarah’s rule to keep the lights off in her room. Mia’s hand yearned to reach for the lamp, but she couldn’t bring herself to do it. She made her way through the dark room to the small bathroom to refresh herself with a hot shower and a change of clothes. After eating a few slices of one of Sarah’s discarded oranges, she placed some gloves and the papers into the shoebox and made her way back down the hallway to check on Sarah. She found her sitting next to Tracy in the corner of the recreation room, visibly upset.

“Is everything okay?” Mia asked, puzzled as to why Sarah wasn’t watching TV anymore.

“Everything’s fine; Sarah’s upset that it’s Evelyn’s turn to watch her shows.” Tracy replied. Sarah slapped her hand on the armrest of her wheelchair, frustrated at Tracy’s response.

“Nobody with good sense watches the *Young and the Restless*! That show is dumb! Evelyn’s blind as a bat! She can’t even see what’s going on! I could be watching my shows and actually see what’s going on!”

Evelyn, who was sitting quietly in front of the TV, turned around in her wheelchair and cut her eyes at Sarah through her thick prescription glasses.

"I can see just fine, you old bat! Now hush up and let me have my turn!"

"Old bat?!" Sarah yelled!

"Ladies!" Tracy scolded. "You both are out of line! Evelyn, turn around and watch the TV. Sarah, you're excused until she's finished."

"She started it!" Sarah grumped.

"Mia, would you be so kind as to take Sarah out to the porch to get some fresh air?"

"Sure, no problem." Mia chuckled under her breath at the two women acting like children. She tucked the shoebox under her arm and pushed Sarah out onto the front porch.

It was another beautiful day, with the sun peeking in and out of the clouds and a fresh fall breeze passing through the trees. Mia locked Sarah's wheelchair in and sat in a rocking chair beside her.

"Sadie, how are you feeling?"

"Don't patronize me. I'm just fine," Sarah pouted. "I can't stand that old goat. She makes my blood boil."

"Well, I could read to you a little more; would that be okay?"

"Guess I don't have a choice. What are we reading?" Sarah groaned and wrapped her shawl around her arms.

"I have Lucinda's story here. I can pick up where we left off." Mia opened the shoe box to show Sarah its contents.

"Where did we leave off?" Sarah asked.

"She just lost her daughter, remember?"

"I remember bits and pieces."

"Did Lucinda ever find her little one after that night? After she marked her?"

Sarah hung her head, knowing the truth to the question was not what she wanted to give.

"No," she replied, "she never did see her daughter again. I like to think that maybe she met her walking down a street one day and didn't recognize her."

Mia paused again, allowing Sarah the time she needed to take Lucinda's words in and find a place for them to rest. She hadn't heard or seen the papers in decades. They were as yellowed and aged as she was.

"The thing that hurts the most," Sarah continued, "is that she's not only gone, but she's almost forgotten. Nobody knows who she is, except me. I'm the only person in the world who remembers what she looked like and what she smelled like; that's a heavy truth to carry around. Nobody cared that she was a good woman, a good mother, and a good soul. Nobody remembers her except me. I'm the only one on this earth who carries her memories in my mind. My mind is fading and losing pieces of her every day. I wish you could know the burden that is placed on a person's heart. To know that dying is more tragic now because I must hold on to her memory."

"You don't have to feel that way," Mia said, smiling. "I have her memories now, too! She's safe with me, and I will never let her memory die."

"That's good to know. It makes things a little easier for me knowing that."

"Are you okay to continue?" Mia asked.

"I'm okay if you are. I need you to keep going. Finish reading for me, please."

Mia agreed and continued with Lucinda's story.

CHAPTER TWENTY-NINE

JAMES

"Won't long 'fore I started tuh feel things. Watchin' Massa Gavin an' Martha tip toe 'round me made me angry. Actin' like I's dumb of what dey done. When I stepped on her little stick dolls dat laid 'round duh field, I feel things. Each one cracked under my feet an' made me feel sad. I feel angry an' sad. Somethin' else be dere. Somethin' else circlin' 'round me. Somethin' dark. Life meant nothin' without her by my side. My mind wanted things tuh go black. For my life tuh end. My heart wanted air tuh stay put in my lungs for duh day I find her. I went on prayin' one day we gonna meet again. Prayin' be duh one thing dat stop me from puttin' heavy rocks in my pockets an' walkin' in duh river.

"I walked slow an' sad for ah long time. No one cared tuh speak tuh me or bother me. Dey let me walk. I walked in circles. I walked in twisted lines. Out an' 'round duh fields. I feel duh flowers dat tried tuh blossom in duh ground, with my fingers. Dey wanted tuh live. Dey hope made me angry. I crushed each one in duh palm of my hands. Bess say I went crazy. Maybe I did tryin' tuh find somethin' dat won't dere anymore.

"I's still walkin' in circles when Massa Gavin come tuh his senses. Like he cured an' lost interest in his whiskey an' gamblin'. He started comin' 'round more in duh daylight, lookin' well an' gettin' color back in his face. We know what he wanted. We know he got somethin' up his sleeve. He come tuh us an' say things lookin' up. He excited 'cause he able tuh bring in ah few new bucks. He made it clear dat we gettin' back tuh breedin'. He start up inspectin' us an' havin Bess check for blood tuh make sure who good tuh breed.

"While I's walkin' an' absent from what dey got goin' on 'round duh plantation, Bess say Massa Gavin done sold off more gals. I ain't even notice. He down tuh me, Mattie, Leah, an' two other gals for breedin'. Bess warned us Massa in need of money an' he busy findin' every way possible tuh get back tuh good fortunes. Same week he come back 'round, he take Mattie an' Leah's boys from dey arms an' put 'em in ah cart tuh be sold. Leah been through it plenty times. She ain't even drop ah tear when her boys screamin' an' callin' for her. Mattie like me. She break down cryin' an' fightin' Massa Gavin tuh get 'em back. She got whipped dat night 'cause she punch Massa in duh back.

"Bess always be our ears an' eyes 'cause Massa Gavin an' Martha talk with her in duh room. Dey ain't care 'cause dey think Bess loyal tuh 'em. Bess hate 'em like us, probably more. Bess come in Mattie's cabin dat night with balm for her back. Me an' Leah tendin' tuh her wounds. Bess upset 'cause she know for sure Massa Gavin lyin'. She say things not lookin' up. She overheard him speakin' with Martha dat mornin'. Dey still low on money an' duh talk of war come up again. Bess say she seen duh fear of God in Massa Gavin's eyes, an' she know it be somethin' real. Massa Gavin wanted tuh give duh breedin' one last go an' sell off duh new babies in duh winter. Den we leave Virginia for safer ground further down South in Mississippi. Dat's where Martha's family be.

"So dat's his plan an' his will. Hearin' dat made me choose my own plan. 'Fore I ever made another slave tuh be sold, or ever felt for someone like I felt for my Little One, my body gonna be tied tuh duh river. Water in my lungs an' stones in my pockets. Made up my mind an' stopped prayin' an' started plannin'. Promised myself dat death gonna be my plan an' my will.

"Duh night come when Massa Gavin say duh bucks comin' tuh duh plantation. I sat waitin' in my cabin. Waitin' for some stranger tuh come in an' climb on me. I's calm. For ah moment, duh calm dat I felt scared me. I felt nothin'. I wanted duh mornin' tuh come. I ain't want tuh get far along with ah baby if this one decide tuh stay in me. I ain't wanna gamble on it peacefully dyin' an' wantin' tuh be buried with duh others. Got tuh move fast, 'fore it start movin' in my belly. I wanted duh mornin' tuh come. I decided dat right 'fore duh sun come up, I's gonna go down in duh water, with rocks in my pockets. Gonna die peacefully 'fore Massa Gavin or someone else get duh chance tuh see me an' stop me.

"Thinkin' so hard 'bout my plan, I ain't have time tuh notice duh door open an' Massa Gavin push someone in. Duh door shut an' I heard Massa's heavy boots walkin' away. I seen ah shadow in duh corner. Walked up an' brought my candle close tuh his face. I tried tuh look in his eyes 'fore I made another move. His head stayed down lookin' at duh ground. He ain't do much talkin'. I seen his eyes. Duh moon only half its size, but even in duh dark, I seen those eyes.

"I say my name Lucinda. He ain't move. I asked him tuh tell me his name. Least he coulda done, 'fore he climb on top ah me. He still ain't move. 'Fore dat night, one dat act like him woulda spooked me. Made me think he crazy or somethin'. This one different. Won't no fight in him tuh harm me. I's calm. He stood dere in duh corner, with his head down an' quiet. I start walkin' 'round duh cabin burnin' ah few more candles. Hopeful he ain't wanna do what Massa sent him tuh do. Hopeful he'd stay put in dat corner an' leave me be. Dem candles lit up duh cabin so I seen him better. His skin dark, like my Little One's. He tall an' slender like ah oak tree startin' tuh take form. Hair thick an' matted like Bess' hair.

Hot wax from duh candle I's holden burnt my fingers, so I placed it down on duh floor for ah moment, 'side my leg an' stood dere, waitin' for him tuh do or say somethin'. His head raised up an' I seen his eyes starin' at my legs. I looked down tuh see what on Earth grabbed his attention. My scar. It lit up in duh candlelight an' his eyes fixed on my skin. Dat's when he come rushin' over tuh me. Dropped tuh his knees an' grabbed my leg, rubbin' my scar an' startin' tuh cry. I seen all types of bucks, while I's breedin'. Mean ones dat treat me bad an' say rude things tuh me. Nice ones dat use manners an' say please. Nasty ones dat do things tuh me dat hurt. All those bucks I been with, but never ah crazy one. I ain't know what tuh do. I's sure he done lost his mind.

"I stood still. I closed my eyes an' waited for him tuh do me duh favor of killin' me so I ain't gotta do it myself. He stayed like dat for ah long time. On his knees, cryin' an' rubbin' my scar. I ain't say ah thing. Not sure what words tuh say tuh comfort him. Didn't even think tuh pull away. I stood dere, an' let him be. I figured he got somethin' heavy on his mind. If my leg did it for him, so be it. Ain't no fight in me tuh stop him.

"Finally, he let my leg go an' stood up tuh his feet. He grabbed my shoulders an' pulled me close. He smelled of old cedar wood an' sweat. I ain't never gonna forget him lookin' me in my eyes. His eyes got water in 'em. Clear water dat ran down duh sides of his face an' on me. He started whisperin' in my ear, sobbin' an' mumblin' 'It's you! It's you!' I's sure dat I ain't never seen him ah day in my life. I know every man dat come tuh my cabin. He not one of 'em. I muttered tuh him askin' who he be an' how he think he know me. He say duh only word he know tuh tell me how close tuh me he be. He wiped his eyes an' whispered tuh me, 'Nitakupata'.

"I froze. Only three people know dat word. My mama, my Little One, an' me. He put his hand in mine, an' sat me down on duh floor. He looked me in my eyes an' start tuh tell me ah story of ah day with pale people an' ah hot unforgivin' sun. He seen ah little gal who danced on ah rock, an' ah beautiful slave woman who grabbed her up an' marked her. He watchin' us duh whole time. Chained tuh ah nearby cart, watchin' dat beautiful slave woman put metal inta duh little gal's leg. Watched while she cried an' screamed. Watched knowin' dat duh mark put on her for ah purpose. Ah purpose he know gonna bring 'em together again one day. He watched duh beautiful slave woman, his wife, an' duh little gal, his daughter, get sold off tuh duh pale people in duh crowd.

"He paused tuh let me get ah few moments tuh understand what he sayin'. He pointed tuh my leg an' say again my mark put dere on purpose, so dat dey daughter be easy tuh find one day. 'I's your daughter.' I say it out loud 'cause it felt unreal. Like one of dem fairy tales Bess tell my Little One.

"So, dere in duh dim light of ah cabin, he found me. He found me broken an' ready tuh die. He found me, lost an' alone. Dat embrace dat come after his story much more than my broken words can say. I wrapped my arms 'round him, cryin' an' releasin' all duh pain an' hurt I done built up. He held me tight, an' repeatin' his words "I found you!" I never in my wildest dreams woulda imagined my daddy comin' tuh me dat night. Dat's duh day I truly start tuh believe in God. I prayed 'fore dat, but I know God heard me now. Dere ain't no explainin' how or why. Tuh know dat if he ain't come tuh me dat night, I woulda been tied tuh duh river dat very next day.

"We sat on dat floor talkin' an' tellin' stories for hours. He say his name James. He start tellin' me 'bout duh plantation he been sold tuh an' duh fields of cotton dat he picked every day. He let me see his hands. Dey littered with rooted scars, fresh blood an' dried up dirt. He tell me 'bout his days an' nights an' how he always believe he gonna see me again. I asked him 'bout my mama, but he tell he ain't seen her since dat day. He sure now dat he found me, dat he gonna find her.

"I tell him all 'bout my Little One. I tell him her name Nitakupata an' marked her like my mama marked me. He overjoyed an' say tuh me 'bout his plans. He asked me if I ever hear anythin' 'bout ah war goin' on. I tell him 'bout Bess an' what she say, but we ain't think much 'bout it 'cause it be ah white folks war. He laughed an' tell me duh truth. He say it 'bout slaves an' dat white folks up North fightin' tuh give us freedom. I 'member I looked at him confused. Freedom? White folks want us tuh have freedom? I start tuh think again dat he crazy. He seen duh disbelief in my eyes an' start tuh tell me all 'bout duh world outside of Massa Gavin's plantation. Stories of soldiers, guns an' abolitionists, all fightin' so dat we know what freedom feel like. He say dat once duh war gone an' over with, we gonna find mama an' my Little One. We gonna be ah family together. His dreams so big dey filled dat little cabin corner tuh corner. I dove inta 'em, believin' every word an' becomin' hopeful dat I's gonna feel freedom like he say.

"Duh night sky filled up with duh sun's light an' we both realized we spent duh whole night talkin'. We spent duh night dreamin' together. I wanted tuh live now, but as quick as we been filled with hope, reality come inta duh cabin an' drained what we built, away. Mornin' come an' Massa Gavin comin' soon, tuh have Bess inspect me an' make sure dat James done what he come tuh do. Massa Gavin ain't take kindly tuh excuses. We sure tuh get ah lashin' if we tried tuh give him any. One way or another, me an' James meant tuh breed."

CHAPTER THIRTY

RESTLESS

"Sadie? Sarah?"

Mia leaned over to rub Sarah's knee. Mia was so engrossed in Lucinda's words that she didn't notice Sarah had fallen asleep. She also didn't notice the sun starting to set and most of the other residents had returned inside the building. Now that she was released from the hold that yellowed pages had over her, she felt a chill in the air. She decided to take Sarah inside to rest in her room. Mia was almost finished packing everything up to head inside when Tracy appeared with a small paper cup in her hand. Mia looked down at its contents to see the blue and black pills again. She knew how much Sarah hated those pills. She didn't want to be the one to deliver them.

"Hi Tracy," Mia whispered. "She's resting."

"I didn't see you two at dinner. Is everything okay?"

"It's dinnertime already?"

Tracy laughed. "She's got you so intrigued that you don't know what time it is?"

"I guess so," Mia replied.

"She's going to put up a fight about these pills, I know it," Tracy muttered. "You can go ahead and get some dinner for yourself in the cafeteria. I'll come grab you once I know she has eaten, taken her meds, and isn't being so argumentative."

"Sounds like a plan. Thank you." Mia stood aside as Tracy took the handles of Sarah's wheelchair and pushed her away. Mia was still deep in thought as she made her way to the cafeteria. She couldn't stop thinking about Lucinda and her father, James. She found a seat at an empty table in the cafeteria and stared at the old shoe box. Mia couldn't look away from it.

Curiosity and suspense wrestled within her. *What happened to Lucinda? What happened to James?* She didn't want to wait for Sarah to get into a good mood and possibly have to delay hearing what happened to Lucinda until the morning. Mia had no interest in food. All she wanted was to continue with the story. Mia's mind raced with discouraging possibilities. She slipped her fingers into the pair of gloves, ready to begin where she had left off.

CHAPTER THIRTY-ONE

SHIFTED

"Seein' duh sun come up more frightenin' for me den for him. I sat on dat floor, wide awake, watchin' him next tuh me. He needed sleep. James been wore out regalin' me with his rich stories 'bout duh places he been. His mind traveled back tuh Mississippi tuh Georgia an' den tuh Virginia dat night, recountin' all of duh things an' people he done seen. He keep sayin' dat he happy now 'cause his travels ain't been in vain. Most of his memories been painful, but dat ain't stop him from fallin' asleep.

"Sleep ain't find me. I sat dere, lookin' at duh door. Waitin' for Massa Gavin tuh come an' take my daddy away. Waitin' for me tuh get inspected an' know we ain't done nothin' dat night. Massa Gavin got ah keen eye for his work. He know when things been done an' when dey ain't. I's sure he 'round duh corner, ready tuh beat me an' James for disobeyin' him.

"James on duh floor, curled up in ah ball, snorin'. I smiled at duh sight of him, but my heart ain't let me love him. Once I loved somethin', it got taken. So, I say tuh myself, I ain't gonna love him. I ain't gonna give him ah place in my heart. My heart still broke from losin' all my babies an' my mama. But some good come from him showin' up in my cabin. I's hopeful dat since he found me in dat dark place, I's gonna find my Little One an' my mama.

"I seen duh sun startin' tuh get much higher than Massa Gavin normally give 'fore he come in. James stayed sleep. I heard others walkin' 'round outside. Some talkin', an' some laughin'. I poked my head out tuh see 'em gathered up ah few feet away. Dey say dat Massa Gavin ain't show up dat mornin'. Bess in duh big house cookin' breakfast for Martha an' duh chillun, so we waited for her tuh come down with news. I let James sleep. Probably duh most sleep he seen in his whole life.

"We all decided dat it be best if we start up our chores while waitin' for Bess. We got tuh work, even duh men, with helpin' us with our baskets an' tendin' tuh duh wash. We quiet. I watched duh sun move dat day, in an' out duh clouds. Still no sign of Massa Gavin come noon. Finally, Bess come walkin' out duh side door from duh big house an' pointed tuh one of duh cabins. It be her signal for everyone tuh gather. We dropped whatever we got in our hands an' made our way tuh Bess. She say dat she hear Martha tellin' duh chillun Massa Gavin been called away for some emergency. She cryin' an' pacin' 'cause some man named Lee surrendered. Bess say 'cause of dat, Massa Gavin spooked real bad an' we gotta move sooner than what he planned. Somethin' must been bad for him tuh leave duh bucks dere with us, unwatched an' free tuh move 'round duh plantation. Bess say Martha want us tuh get tuh duh big house an' start packin' everythin', so we ready when Massa Gavin return.

"So, we worked an' we waited. Each day we keep lookin' at duh dirt road waitin' for Massa Gavin tuh come with news. We stood on needles, dumb of what duh world got goin' on.

Martha started actin' funny. Massa Gavin done went away again an' left her tuh oversee us all. 'Fore dat day, she lax, knowin' dat we ain't have any desire tuh run. Somethin' different now. She start pacin' 'round with Massa Gavin's gun an' talkin' tuh herself. She ain't wash herself an' she fine with walkin' 'round in duh same ol' smelly dress. She'd fight off Bess every time she try tuh get her tuh duh basin. Duh chillun still played an' acted like nothin' wrong, but we all seen Martha an' we know somethin' wrong. Duh bucks dat Massa brought in, stayed. No one come for 'em. James stayin' be duh only thing dat took my mind from duh uneasy feelin' dat stay heavy over duh plantation.

"Three moons come up an' down in duh sky from when James come in my cabin tuh duh day Massa Gavin come home. Three moons we spent together. My happiness come back again. James stayed by my side, while I worked an' while I slept. By day, he tell me things he learned from his travels. He showed me 'round duh fields an' teach me 'bout plants an' trees. He teach me how dey help an' how dey hurt. Bess teach me some, but James teach me more. James duh one dat teach me 'bout mint plants. Showed me how dey good for chewin' an' healin'. At night, he tell me stories. He tell me dat his last Massa been kind an' showed him how tuh read an' write ah few words. He say he'd show me. I never dreamed of readin' an' writin'. James say it be important for me tuh learn. I asked what "Nitakupata" meant. He ain't know. He say my mama born an' lived in Africa, but he born on ah plantation an' never learned how tuh speak duh words like she did. He took sticks an' wrote in duh dirt, quick tuh kick away what he done. He showed me simple words like cat, dog, food, happy, sad an' love. Dat's duh first time I seen duh word "love". I hear it from time tuh time, but I never seen it. Such ah small word carryin' so much weight. I know James loved me an' eventually I loved him back.

"Duh day Massa come home, I woke tuh duh others stirrin' an' movin' outside my cabin. James already awake an' at duh door watchin' 'em. He looked at me an' say dat Massa Gavin's horse out front duh big house. He seen some other horses dat got blue painted saddles on dey backs. He ain't sure if Massa Gavin comin' down from duh house soon. Everyone start gettin' dressed for work dat day. I jumped up an' got myself dressed. Massa Gavin sent Bess down ah few moments later tuh call us all tuh duh front porch. I seen on Bess face dat she troubled. We made our way tuh duh front of duh big house. Massa Gavin an' some strange men standin' on duh porch. Dey dressed in blue caps an' blue wool coats. James pulled me close tuh him. We all waitin' on Massa Gavin tuh speak. His face look all twisted an' mean.

"He yelled out tuh us dat duh war over now. He tell us dat we all got what we wanted. Duh strange men standin' with him got back on dey horses an' say dat dey be back in duh mornin' tuh make sure we gone. Massa Gavin waited 'til dey well off duh plantation tuh speak again. He say we tuh leave his home at once. We all looked 'round at each other, confused 'bout what he mean. We all grown up on dat plantation. Dere ain't any other place tuh call home. Dat's duh only home we know. Massa Gavin got upset dat his words fell on deaf ears. We waited for him tuh make sense of what he sayin'. So, he did. He pulled duh pistol from his side an' pointed tuh duh sky an' fired. It scared me an' James near death. Heard Mattie scream from behind us. He screamin' dat we got tuh leave at once. Yelled out dat if we ain't leave, he gonna shoot us. James grabbed my hand an' pulled me away. He told me tuh walk with him an' he'd make things clear later. He looked at duh others an' told 'em tuh come on. We all started walkin' towards duh dirt road. James started sayin' tuh us dat we all free now an' tuh rejoice! Dis duh day we all waited for, worked hard for an' prayed for. Not knowin' where we goin' or how we gonna get dere. We walked away, an' for ah moment's time, I seen dat everythin' dat James been dreamin' of, finally happenin'. He not only free, but free an' with me.

"We heard Massa Gavin yellin' from duh porch. Yellin' like when he come home full of whiskey. He shot his gun in duh air again, yellin' out dat we wasn't movin' fast like he want. James grabbed my arm an' we started runnin' towards duh road. Everyone took off after dat, goin' in different directions, tryin' tuh make sure dey stay clear from Massa Gavin's bullets. James' breath start gettin' heavier. Duh tall grass keep whippin' cross my legs, makin' me itch. James looked down at me smilin', huffin' out of his mouth dat we almost tuh duh main road.

"Den I hear another shot. James got ah tight grip on my hand but it went loose. I watched him fall tuh duh ground. I stopped an' yelled for him tuh get up. I's sure he tripped an' fallen on somethin' in duh tall grass. But he ain't move. He ain't move. I rushed over tuh him tuh find his once clean shirt, covered in blood. Massa Gavin done shot him, right through duh shoulder. I ain't have time tuh think. I ain't have time tuh cry. I only got time tuh pull him in duh woods, gettin' us both out of Massa Gavin's sight. Not sure how long I tugged an' pulled him. I know when I looked up, I seen we deep enough in an' we safe.

"I cleared ah space in duh leaves an' dirt for James. He keep moanin' an' spittin' up blood. I helped deliver ah few babies on duh plantation, so I knew ah few things 'bout wounds an' healin'. I worked quick, rippin' up some of my dress an' his pants tuh cover duh bloody hole in his shoulder. Got some tinder an' did my best tuh start ah small fire 'fore night fall. Dere ain't much more I's able tuh do. Won't possible tuh go back tuh duh cabin an' get duh ointments he needed. No needle tuh patch him up. Everyone dat been standin' with us done run off, an' left me an' James tuh fend for ourselves. I's prayin' dat duh fire keep him warm an' duh bandages keep him from bleedin' out."

CHAPTER THIRTY-TWO

PROMISES

"Excuse me, Miss Briggs?"

A soft pat on the shoulder jerked Mia out of her trance. She wiped her face with the sleeve of her shirt, unaware that tears were falling from her eyes. Turning in her chair, she found a male nurse standing behind her, smiling. He was dressed in blue scrubs that matched the color of the old hallway walls. There was a certain Southern twang in his voice, and his bronzed skin smelled of tanning oil.

"Hi, I'm Scott. Sorry to interrupt your reading, ma'am, but Tracy wanted me to come and speak with you. She went home for the evening, but wanted to let you know that Sarah's in her room resting now."

"Oh, okay, that's great." Mia continued wiping her face and collecting her thoughts.

"Tracy also wanted you to be aware that we did a vitals check on Sarah, and her blood pressure was a little high. We gave her some additional medication, and she should be good to go."

"Can I go into the room with her?"

"Yes, of course!" said Scott, running his fingers through his hard-gelled hair. "Tracy explained your situation, and I know all about Sarah's condition. I think it's great that you're staying with her."

Mia smiled, carefully folding the yellowed pages of Lucinda's story back into the shoe box.

Making her way back to Sarah's room, she noticed the empty hallways and closed doors around the building. She had stayed in the cafeteria much longer than she anticipated. She once again made her way to the door marked 129 and went inside. The smell of fresh mint filled her senses again, and she instantly felt at ease. She peeked into Sarah's room, unable to see anything at first in the dark space.

"Sadie? Are you awake?" Mia whispered. A frail voice replied to her from the darkness.

"I'm up, but you better make it quick. Come in and sit," Sarah muttered.

Mia quickly took her place on the edge of Sarah's bed.

"How are you feeling?"

"I'm old," she grumbled. "That's how I'm feeling." Sarah tried turning her body around towards Mia, but the aches and pains prevented her from doing so. She muttered a few curse words and laid back down.

"You don't have to move," Mia said, rubbing Sarah's legs.

"Where am I?" Sarah moaned.

"You're in your room, in your bed."

"And you're Mia, right?"

"Yes, ma'am. I'm your granddaughter, Mia."

Mia's heart sank, remembering what Tracy had told her about Sarah's condition.

"Good, then I haven't lost my mind yet." Sarah chuckled, but Mia could tell she was exhausted.

"Get some rest. I'll come check on you in the morning." Mia got up to leave the room, but Sarah called out to her to stop.

"Why are you sad? What's wrong?" Sarah asked.

"I'm not sad, just a little tired," Mia hesitantly replied.

Mia quietly waited, hoping that Sarah would look past her vague reply. She wanted to talk about Lucinda and where she had left off, but she also didn't want to make Sarah feel uncomfortable about it. "You've been reading more of Lucinda's story, haven't you?" Sarah found the words she wanted to say, startling Mia with her blunt response. Mia felt tears welling up in the corners of her eyes, and she sat back down in the corner of the bed with Sarah.

"I...I...I've been reading since we came in from outside. I read up to the part where James got shot, and Lucinda dragged him into the woods."

Sarah was silent. She remembered her own emotions as she wrote Lucinda's words down. She saw strength in Lucinda, never once showing weakness or emotion. Each time something happened, all Sarah wanted was to cry for Lucinda. Sarah wanted to hug Lucinda and let her know she cared, but the moment never came.

She became emotional in the moment with Mia, realizing she'd never see Lucinda again except in her dreams by the water. She could tell that the words affected Mia, too, and felt sorry for her. Ignoring her aches and pains, she sat up in her bed and pulled Mia into her chest. Mia let go of the tears she was holding back, pressing her face into Sarah's nightgown.

"I had to watch my own mother slowly die in front of me. Lucinda had to do the same, but with her father. You make me a promise right now, child. Promise me you'll go home and forgive your mother. Do it for those of us who wish we could still see our loved ones. Don't spend the rest of your life hating her just because she lost the will to love. Promise me you'll forgive her and move on with your life."

"I promise." Mia sniffled.

Sarah shushed her and kept patting her head. Mia breathed in Sarah's deep, earthy scent and wanted to stay in her arms for as long as Sarah would allow.

"No more talking," Sarah whispered to Mia. "Lie down and go to sleep."

There were no windows in Sarah's bedroom to let the sun in to greet Mia the next morning. She was nestled comfortably between Sarah's warm body and the cold plastered wall, unaware that the day had started without her. Her heavy eyes were deep in sleep but fluttered when the delicious smell of buttery pancakes filled the room. Mia's senses danced with excitement, and she rose out of bed, determined to locate where the smell was coming from. She could tell Sarah was still fast asleep. She gently scooted her body to the edge of the bed and tiptoed out of the room. After splashing some water on her face from the kitchen sink and checking her appearance in a small mirror on the table, Mia made her way to the hallway. The delicious aroma carried her down to the cafeteria, where she found Tracy preparing pancakes over a large, hot griddle.

"Well, good morning, Mia!" Tracy said.

"Good morning, Tracy. Your cooking smells absolutely amazing!" Mia looked down at the griddle, licking her lips. She could see six round pancakes bubbling on top of a thin layer of hot butter.

"These are my world-famous pancakes," Tracy proclaimed. "I cook them every Sunday for everyone in the building. Keeps folks happy and keeps me employed!" Tracy could see Mia's desire for one of her pancakes in her eyes. She chuckled at the sight of Mia's mouth open and watering. Tracy gave in and slid a fresh pancake from her pile onto a paper plate and handed it to Mia, who didn't hesitate as she folded the pancake up like a taco and shoved it in her mouth.

"Maybe you'll put some syrup on the next one." Tracy laughed.

"I didn't eat anything last night. I'm starving!" Tracy slid a few more pancakes onto Mia's plate and handed her a bottle of syrup.

"You have the same clothes on as you did yesterday. Had a rough night with Sarah?"

"Not really; I fell asleep and didn't get a chance to eat or get changed." Mia sighed and shoved another piece of pancake into her mouth.

"Did Scott come and tell you about her vitals?"

"Yes, he did. He said everything was okay after you all gave her some medication for her high blood pressure, though."

Tracy shook her head. She huffed and put down the spatula. "Everything was not okay. Scott's always doing that. Her blood pressure was really high yesterday, so we gave her some pretty heavy medication. Did she seem off last night when you spoke with her?"

"No, but she did hug me," Mia replied.

"Well, knowing Sarah, I would classify that as being off. I'm going to keep an eye on her throughout the day today, just to be sure she doesn't have any reactions to the medication we gave her."

"Okay. Can I take her some pancakes?"

"Of course you can. Come back if you want more. I'll be here cooking for another hour or so. After I'm finished, I'll come in and check on Sarah."

Mia watched Tracy pile several fluffy pancakes onto another plate for her to take. A feeling of sadness came over her as she watched.

"I don't know how I'm going to get the strength to leave you and Sarah," Mia said. "I have to get back home soon. I have a deadline to meet and haven't even begun working on it. Before I leave, I wanted to say thank you, Tracy, for being so nice to me. Being here with Sarah has changed my life! I feel so much stronger and confident now when I'm with her. She makes me feel loved."

"You're becoming the little sister I never wanted!" Tracy laughed. "I'm glad to get the chance to know you, Mia. Now go on and try not to eat all those pancakes before Sarah gets a chance to eat!"

Mia skipped down the hallway with her full plate of pancakes and a smile on her face. She came to the door to find it wide open and Scott inside the room, pushing Sarah from her bedroom to the kitchen table.

"Oh, hey there, Mia!" Scott said.

"Hi Scott. Is everything okay?"

"Yeah, everything's fine. I just came to take Sarah's vitals and was taking her to the table to eat breakfast. Looks like you beat me to it." Scott pushed Sarah closer to the table and covered her lap with a throw blanket.

"Thanks, Scott. I can take it from here. Tracy said she would be in later to check on her again."

Scott nodded and made his way out of the room. Mia sat down at the table across from Sarah. She looked into Sarah's face and realized she wasn't moving. She seemed to be in a trance.

"Sadie…are you okay?" she asked, extending her hand out across the table, hoping Sarah would want to hold it, but she didn't move. Sarah stared straight ahead as if she could see nothing at all. Mia hurried into the hallway to catch Scott. She called out to him, and he jogged back to see what had happened.

"Scott, what's wrong with her? She's just sitting there staring at me. She isn't talking or moving."

"No, no, Mia. It's the medication she took. It can cause symptoms like that. She's okay; she's going to be in and out of a stupor for a little while."

As she remembered Tracy's remark about Scott underestimating situations, Mia rolled her eyes but still thanked him for letting her know. She would stay calm and not cause a scene, but she'd get a second opinion from Tracy when she came to check on Sarah. She closed the door behind her and went back to the table with Sarah.

"Sadie, are you hungry?" Mia asked, trying to stay calm. Sarah said nothing. Mia pushed the plate of fresh pancakes towards Sarah.

She watched as a cloud of fragrant steam rose up into Sarah's face. Sarah looked down at the pancakes but remained silent.

Mia cut up a few pancakes for Sarah. She slowly lifted one to Sarah's mouth, but she didn't respond. Mia wanted to cry, but she knew Sarah wouldn't allow it. She decided the best thing to do would be to continue reading to Sarah. She prayed that Lucinda's words would be enough to bring Sarah back to life.

CHAPTER THIRTY-THREE

FREEDOM

"I sat an' tended tuh his wound. He keep spittin' up blood an' whisper words I ain't understand. No food, only cloudy water from duh stream. Days of cryin' out tuh God for help. Nights of bein' scared tuh sleep. I feared dat Massa Gavin or ah patty roller gonna see duh light from our fire an' come kill us both. I's helpless, watchin' him die.

"On ah night when duh moon up high, fillin' duh sky with light, I seen his eyes wide open an' his body still. I went over, rubbin' his face. He ain't move. Duh blood from his mouth stale. I ain't hear duh whispers either. I laid my head on his cold chest an' cried myself tuh sleep dat night. I slept right dere with his lifeless body. I felt calm with duh thought dat he finally free. Mornin' come an' I got tuh work diggin' ah hole big enough for his body. My hands cracked an' bled in duh cold hard ground. While I's diggin', I seen dat we near where I buried my babies. It comforted me tuh know James 'side 'em, all of 'em free.

"I finally got him in duh dirt. Covered him up good an' cleaned my hands in duh water. I sat, tryin' tuh think. My only thoughts been of James an' watchin' him die. I ain't thought of much else. Now he gone an' my mind open an' empty. My mind ah blank piece of paper waitin' for feelin's tuh come on in an' fill up duh spaces.

"First, duh boilin' come risin' up in me again. Same boilin' I got duh mornin' I seen my Little One been taken from me. Duh boilin' didn't have time tuh root 'cause I start tuh feel ah different kinda boilin'. Ah boilin' of anger an' rage dat sit heavy inside my broken heart. I ain't never felt dat kinda boilin' 'fore. Even after every beatin' Massa Gavin give tuh me, duh shavins from Martha, an' even duh pain of dem bucks on top ah me. Dat boilin' colored my heart dark shades of red.

"I 'member my eyes pourin' tears. Tears for James. Tears for my mama. Tears for my babies. All dat rage an' anger dat been boilin' up on duh inside of me pointed tuh one name. One reason why my life turned sour. Massa Gavin. He duh reason for it all. He duh reason I got no family. Everyone I loved now gone, an' it be all his doin'.

"I 'member walkin' in duh dark towards duh plantation. I know I's crazy tuh go back. Won't nothin' in my hands. Nothin' tuh use if Massa Gavin tried tuh come after me. I ain't know what tuh do when I got dere. Maybe yell. Maybe cry. Maybe set duh whole plantation on fire. My feet won't my own in dat moment. My body start movin' but it won't by my doin'.

"I got tuh duh front of duh big house. I seen him in duh light of duh moon. He slumped in his favorite chair lookin' at me, sayin' nothin', like he know what bring me tuh him. He looked up with his whiskey filled eyes an' I seen him clearly. Ah broken man, now livin' ah worthless life without us tuh make him wealthy.

"I looked 'round for Martha or anyone one else, but duh porch empty. Rage lifted duh souls of my feet up dem steps.

Found myself standin' right in front ah him, lookin' down on him in his chair. He so drunk, he ain't even stand up. He seen my eyes filled with tears. He laughed. Laughed sayin' he thought he shot me. Thought I's dead. He laughed sayin' I must be ah ghost. He took ah few more sips of his whiskey an' laid his heavy head back in duh chair. All my pain an' all he destroyed, he found amusin'. He laughed. He laughed at me. He laughed at my scars. He laughed at my black skin. He laughed at my pain. He kept on laughin'.

"So, I laughed too. I laughed thinkin' of me killin' him right dere, on duh porch. Shootin' him dead like he did my daddy. Dat laugh made duh boilin' worse. We both laughin' like two ol' crazy fools. I seen his head laid back in duh chair an' his neck clear tuh me in duh moonlight. I grabbed duh whiskey bottle from his limp hand. I cracked it on duh side of duh chair an' pieces went flyin' everywhere. My hand got dat neck of duh bottle gripped tight. 'Fore he even got ah chance tuh realize duh broken glass pressed tuh his neck, I dug it deep in his skin. I watched him grab his neck an' he dropped on tuh duh ground. Hunched over an' garglin' up his blood in pain. He ain't able tuh scream with all dat blood flowin' out his mouth.

"I stood dere watchin' Massa Gavin slowly die, like I watched James. I watched him rock back an' forth reachin' out for someone or somethin' tuh help him. I laughed. Poor Massa Gavin. His white skin ain't gonna save him now. Won't even afraid of Martha comin' down tuh find what I done. I know dat I's truly free. I walked off dat porch with ah smile on my face. I walked down dat dark dirt road an' inta town, covered in blood an' not ah care in my mind. I's free an' felt free for duh first time. It feel good, just like James promised."

CHAPTER THIRTY-FOUR

ASHAMED

Tracy slipped quietly into the room while Mia was reading. Mia was so absorbed by the words that she didn't notice Tracy or the medication cart she wheeled in behind her. Mia continued on as Tracy stood over Sarah, taking her vitals. She lifted Sarah's arm, gently wrapped a large blue strap around it and pumped air into the black bulb. Tracy shook her head at the sight of her world-famous pancakes still sitting in front of Sarah. The steam was gone, and the pancakes were now cold and mushy.

As Mia finished the words on the page, she looked up at Sarah. She was still staring blankly ahead, with her eyes now fixed on the scenery outside the window. Mia placed down the pages of Lucinda's story and breathed a sigh of relief.

"Serves him right!" she proclaimed. "I'm glad she killed that evil bastard."

"I see Sarah's potty mouth is rubbing off on you." Tracy chuckled.

"I'm sorry, Tracy. I was reading to Sarah, and I got caught up in the moment."

"What on earth is that you're reading to her?"

"Still the same story from before. You came in on the good part." Mia smiled.

"Some woman slitting a man's throat is the *good part*? How morbid!"

"I'll make sure to fill you in later about everything. It's a lot to take in."

"I'll take your word for it," Tracy said. She unwrapped Sarah's arm and took her temperature. After jotting a few notes down in a small notepad, Tracy pushed the cart back to the door.

"I see she didn't eat anything this morning. Could you please try to get her to eat one of those oranges or a pastry from the table? If she doesn't eat soon, I'll have to get an IV in her, and trust me, that's not something we want to do. Last time we put one in her, she tried to bite me!"

"The last thing I need is her trying to bite anyone," Mia groaned. "I'll make sure she eats something." Mia waved goodbye to Tracy as she slipped out the door.

Mia pulled an orange from the fruit bowl and peeled it for Sarah. Sarah didn't budge, even when Mia placed the juicy piece of fruit down in front of her. Her eyes were still glued to the window. Mia sighed and stood up, taking the cold plate of pancakes to the trash can. She had her back turned to Sarah when, suddenly, Sarah began to speak. Her voice was frail and cracked, but she pushed out what she had to say anyway. Mia spun around and rushed to Sarah's side. She was overjoyed to hear something come from Sarah. Anything to let her know she hadn't lost her. She placed her hand on Sarah's shoulder and smiled.

"What did you say, Sadie? I could barely hear you."

"You shouldn't say things like that," she grunted, trying to project her voice.

"What do you mean, Sadie? I'm glad you're talking, though. I know you're probably not hungry, but I—"

Sarah cut Mia off, pulling her shoulder away from her grasp. Her face became twisted again. Mia sat back down in her chair and let Sarah finish what she was trying to say.

"You. You shouldn't say things like that. That you're glad that Lucinda did what she did."

Mia looked puzzled. She wasn't sure what she meant.

"I don't understand why you wouldn't be happy, too. She killed him. He deserved it! He killed James. He whipped her and made her do horrible things. He deserved to die. Lucinda was even happy that she killed him."

"You don't understand, child." Sarah kept her eyes fixated on the window. She began to feel a moment of clarity, but the strain of her fatigue was getting to her.

"You've never seen hate and the reality of racism the way I have. Lucinda was only happy because she gained a sense of freedom she never had before. I could and can still see what you and she could not—the truth. I saw what the truth would do, and I became terrified. As I was going to hand over my story to Claudette, I realized that if I told Lucinda's story and told the world what she did, there was a good chance Lucinda could be punished or, worse, killed."

A look of confusion came across Mia's face. She didn't understand how Sarah could assume that Lucinda would've been in any danger.

"Killed? What do you mean, killed? She did what she did long before she told you. Why would anyone want to kill her when she was so old? His family was long gone by then."

"Mia," Sarah said, "I've seen old men hung from trees. I've seen young children pulled from rivers with their faces smashed in. I've written about these things for years. I've seen what they do to Black people who defy the rules. Killing a White man is something that no one would forgive. Lucinda broke a rule that every Black person knew would lead to death. She was brave enough to tell me, but I was terrified of telling the world. She was very much alive when I went to turn those pages in. I even had plans to go back and see her again. But after I made my decision, I was too afraid to face her. I was too ashamed to let her know I failed her. I couldn't risk anyone finding out what she'd done and putting her in danger. I couldn't bear the thought of someone reading what she told me and punishing her. She'd been punished enough. I made my choice, and I regret it to this day."

Mia, who once was elated, was now ashamed of her moment of ignorance. She hadn't given it a second thought after reading Lucinda's words. Now, she sat with her tail between her legs.

"I'm sorry."

"Don't apologize. I don't expect you or anyone else to understand."

"Do you want me to finish the rest?" Mia said, lifting the yellowed pages up in front of her.

"The rest of what? There's more?"

"Yes. There are a few more pages here."

Sarah looked around the room, trying to remember what else was there on the pages. She couldn't remember the words she had written, but she knew she wanted to listen. The fog was setting in again.

"Go on, child. Read them to me."

CHAPTER THIRTY-FIVE

MARY

"Mornin' come, an' duh boilin' in me died. Not sure where I slept dat night or how I got dere. No one seen me walkin' wit my dress full ah Massa Gavin's blood. Some folk feel strange after seein' death. I ain't feel strange. I ain't feel nothin'. No guilt an' no sad tears tuh taste. Got good sleep dat night. I woke an' stretched myself out. I wuz lookin' 'round for somethin' familiar so my mind know where my body gone.

"Found I's in ah small backyard. It be fenced in an' ah little gray house, ah few feet away from where I stood. I brushed myself off an' looked 'round for ah way out. I needed tuh run 'fore someone found me all bloody an' know what I done. When I got one foot over dat wooden fence, ah squeaky little voice called out tuh me from one of duh windows of duh gray house. Ah gal, who I ain't see, yelled at me, askin' what I's doin' on her property. My foot still on duh fence an' I hurried tuh make it over 'fore she say another word. She swung open duh back door an' pointed ah pistol at me. I froze, scared for my life. Blood in me ran cold, especially after seein' what Massa Gavin done with ah pistol like dat.

"She be ah young white gal with skin pale like Martha's. Her long blonde hair all messy an' bunched up on her shoulders. She got bright blue eyes dat look tuh be sweet but got boilin' in 'em. Standin' tall an' fearless, she pointed dat gun right at me. She askedagain what I's doin' on her property. I's so terrified, I couldn't speak. She seen fear in my eyes. She lowered her gun, an' looked at me. She asked my name. I's barely able tuh get out duh word, Lucinda. I watched her lookin' me up an' down, inspectin' my bloody dress. I say duh only lie dat come tuh me. Told her I killed ah chicken. Told her 'bout ah big ol' chicken dat put up ah fight an' prayed she believed my lie. I apologized tuh her for bein' dere an' asked her kindly if she let me leave with my life.

"She put duh pistol in her apron an' told me her name Mary. Mary Brock. She somethin' called ah abolitionist. I 'membered my daddy tellin' me 'bout white folks like her. Good, God-fearin' white folks who wanted tuh see us set free. All dat ain't matter tuh me in dat moment. All dat matter dat she white with ah gun an' I's black an' trespassin'. Mary ain't shoot me though. She been fine tuh do so 'cause duh law on her side, but she kind tuh me. Much kinder den any white person I'd met 'fore dat day. She seen duh fear an' hunger all wrapped up in my eyes. She feel sorry for me. She say I's welcome tuh come in an' eat breakfast. All those days without food made me weak. I ain't argue or try tuh say no. Ain't help I smelled tuh high heaven. Mary took me in, washed me up, give me clothes tuh wear, an' sat me down tuh eat.

"While shovin' hot biscuits an' porridge in my mouth, she sat 'side me an' started tuh cry. I looked up from my meal an' seen her eyes filled with tears. I ain't care much why she cryin'. I start tuh thinkin' her white troubles never gonna match duh hell I'd seen. She all alone an' I's probably duh only person who gonna listen. I tried tuh be kind, so I asked her why she cryin'. She got herself up an' start pacin' duh floor, tellin' me her story.

"She say she got no one tuh talk tuh. Everyone in town treat her unkind 'cause dey know she ah abolitionist. Dey blamed her for dey dead loved ones, who died in duh war. She say she been sad ah long time 'cause she lost her beloved husband, Edward, in duh war. He gone off tuh fight with dem Yankee soldiers. She happy once with Edward in duh house with her. Her belly got big with ah baby when Edward gone tuh war. She say when news come dat he dead, she fell on duh floor wrong an' lost duh baby. I's troubled dat ah white woman upset like dat. She able tuh come an' go as she pleased, buy anythin' she want, an' never be forced tuh do duh things I's forced tuh do. But she got ah pain as real as mine. No black an' white at dat moment. Our pain be duh same color.

"I reached out my hand tuh her an' told her my story, but I made sure tuh leave out how Massa Gavin died. Everythin' else I give tuh her. I told her 'bout duh plantation an' what we forced tuh do. Told her 'bout Martha an' showed her my bald head. Told her 'bout my Little One an' how I's gonna find her one day. Told her 'bout my daddy an' how he died. Ended with duh lie 'bout duh chicken tuh keep coverin' my tracks. Mary ain't say ah word while I told her my story. I seen she saddened by my words. After I say everythin' dat trouble me, she say it would bring her joy if I stay an' be her maid. Ask me if I would help her 'round duh house 'cause dat fall she took hurt her leg an' she in pain. She ain't have money tuh pay me, but she got shelter an' food. She kind so I decided tuh stay. Ain't nowhere else I's able tuh go. Mary took me tuh ah small spare room down in duh basement. Dat basement damp an' dark, but dat's where I lay my head. I stayed sleep all mornin' an' on in duh night. Best sleep of my life.

"Next mornin', I woke tuh duh smell of hot biscuits an' made my way tuh duh kitchen. I greeted Mary with ah smile, but she look troubled. She pointed tuh ah chair at duh table an' told me tuh sit. I got worried but I sat like she told me an' she went on makin' breakfast. She put ah plate of biscuits an' porridge in front of me an' sat down tuh her own. She looked at me an' say dat two men an' duh sheriff just left her porch. Dey askin' if she got any news 'bout ah murder. She say dat ah man named Gavin Hughes been killed. His neck been cut clean open an' no one seen or heard ah thing. His poor wife found him duh next mornin'. Duh men now out lookin' for duh man who done it.

"Mary look up at me with heavy eyes. She reminded me of when I come tuh her, covered in blood. Kept my head down lookin' at my food an' keepin' my eyes from hers. I's afraid if she looked in 'em, she sure tuh know duh truth. I's sure she gonna turn me in. I looked tuh duh door, waitin' for duh men tuh come in an' take me away. Dey sure tuh hang me. My fear made it impossible tuh say anythin'. My silence made me guilty.

"Mary looked at me an' told me tuh eat for my food get cold. She say she know duh kinda business Mr. Gavin Hughes been part of. She heard duh stories an' I confirmed it all. She sad hearin' duh things he forced us tuh do. She say dat duh men gone now. She pointed tuh duh fireplace dat got ah fire goin'. My eyes got big when I seen my dress wrapped 'round duh wood in duh flames. Ain't know what tuh say. Mary saved my life twice now. She seen duh shock all on my face, but all she tellin' me tuh do is eat my food for it get cold.

"She never bring up Massa Gavin again after dat day. Heard talk 'round town dat everyone sure he been killed 'cause of his gamblin' debts. Dem men catch up tuh one of Massa Gavin's foes who say many ah time dat he gonna kill Gavin Hughes 'cause he stole from him. Heard dey hung dat man for killin' Massa Gavin. Dat's why my heart heavy. Dat he hangin' from ah tree, innocent of what I really done. Wanted tuh come clean an' face my fate, but I never got duh nerve tuh confess. Never wanted anyone tuh die for my sin. From what I heard in passin' years, Martha sold off everythin' dey owned an' moved back tuh Mississippi tuh be with family. Dat be duh end of Massa Gavin an' his breedin' plantation.

"From den on, I lived in Mary's company. She never got ah husband after Edward died, an' I ain't choose tuh find out what life be like elsewhere. We stuck together, widow an' slave. We both marked. I's safe with Mary. I ain't stray from duh protection she give tuh me. I spent my days hidin' in duh house. I keep duh house clean. Cooked her meals like Bess show me. Washed her linens an' tended tuh her garden outback. I ain't go far. I's always afraid of goin' out an' havin' people find out what I done. My bloody dress been burned, but I still felt Massa Gavin's blood on me. Felt dat innocent man's blood on me like Massa's. Ain't matter how many baths I took. Ain't matter how many times I scrubbed my hands till dey raw. Dey blood soaked in my skin. Even started havin' nightmares 'bout it. Heard his voice garglin' an' watchin' him die. Seen dat man swingin' from ah tree, lookin' me in my eyes, knowin' I done killed Massa an' not him.

"Time went on, an' I tried tuh do away with my guilt. Duh nightmares stopped an' my skin got clean. I got pleasure walkin' outside in duh yard. Pickin' flowers an' watchin' duh clouds move cross duh sky. I start walkin' tuh town with Mary an' doin' her shoppin' with her. I breathed duh air. I stuck my toes in duh dirt. I's free.

"Mary treat me good. Never able thank her enough for her love an' kindness. She even try tuh teach me how tuh read an' write. She always sayin' knowledge for ah woman be ah powerful weapon against any ignorant man. She start off slow teachin' me. She started with A an' worked her way tuh Z. She read me poetry an' helped me understand duh beauty in things. She laugh when I say words wrong.

Mary teach me 'bout God an' Jesus. She come home one day from church wit ah new song dey singin' an' she teach me 'bout ah woman in dah Bible who lost everythin' an' still say all is well. Mary say I's just like dat woman cause I lost my momma, my daddy an' my babies, but I ain't let dat stop me from livin'. "It is well with my soul" she always singin' 'round duh house an' got me steadfast on believin' dem words myself. She say our sins been washed away an' all is well with our souls!

Things went on dat way for years, an' me an' Mary got old, side by side.

"Den Mary got sick. I start tuh be more of ah nurse for her den ah maid. She started achin' real bad an' limpin' 'round duh house. Tried my best tuh save her life way she saved mine. I ain't wanna see her go, but she know her time comin'. Told me tuh be strong. Mary smart as dey come an' she know white folks in town ain't bout tuh let me stay in her house, no matter what papers she signed. One day, we's on duh way tuh see ah friend of hers an' dat's when we seen dis here cottage. Mary loved it. Bought it for me an' died dat same week. She's buried in ah white's only cemetery. I ain't even permitted tuh see her grave or pay my respects.

"I been here, keepin' tuh myself since den. I only seen Mattie from duh plantation. Not sure what happen tuh Leah, Bess or duh others. Never did find my Little One. Looked high an' low. Asked some ah duh freed folk 'round town. No one seen ah gal with ah scar on her leg. Pray every day she somewhere, happy an' free. Pray she know I tried tuh find her. Pray she know I love her.

"As for what I done tuh Massa Gavin dat night, I pray dat God forgive me. I done carried dis secret for so long, it be ah part of me. Make me feel unworthy of things like love an' forgiveness. Never did tell Mary or anyone else duh truth. I know she know duh truth of what I done but sometimes I like tuh think maybe she believed my lie. Dat she imagined me an' dat chicken fightin', with me comin' out covered in blood.

"Dat's my life. Everythin' dat I care tuh 'member, I shared. I lived ah simple life. I ain't got titles, fame or fortune. I hope dat my words give way for grace tuh be given over me. For duh truth tuh be told an' duh world tuh know what I done. I hope dat maybe, somehow, dis here story find my Little One, an' let her know dat she always been ah part of me. Don't know who gonna read my story, but hope whoever dey are, dey get ah little stronger, knowin' it is well. No matter what, it is well."

CHAPTER THIRTY-SIX

ABSOLUTION

The end.

It was over. Lucinda's words settled like the thick dust covering Mary's dormant books. Every word, every emotion, every memory was now passed on to Mia.

Thoughts of Lucinda's indelible words bound to the yellowed pages circled Mia throughout the night like a moth unable to release itself from the captivating grip of a flame. The closer she got, the more painful it all became. Mia could feel the sharp, heated sting of the jagged metal digging into Lucinda's skin. Her body became consumed with a hollow ache while she watched Lucinda's cold, bloody fingers dig into the hardened earth to bury her children and James by the water. Rage consumed her, watching Gavin laugh in her face, but turned to sweet vengeance as his whiskey-steeped blood soaked into the tattered fabric of Lucinda's dress. The room soon filled with the savory aroma of Mary's fresh homemade biscuits, wrapping Mia in warmth and unconditional kindness. She felt connected to every word, standing beside Lucinda, watching every unimaginable moment unfold right before her eyes. Moments she knew were so raw and unsaturated that it broke her heart, realizing the world had never known their existence.

Mia suddenly sat up, startled by an astounding thought that crossed her mind. *Unsaturated moments.* She studied it for a moment to ensure it was plausible. She couldn't believe it, but there it was, showing her what had been there the whole time. The one thing that would give Sarah the peace she longed for. The one thing that could set Sarah and Lucinda free from their guilt and save herself in the process. Mia's heart leapt with excitement. There was no time to wait. She hopped up from the couch and slipped quietly into Sarah's room, sitting on the edge of her bed. She whispered good morning a few times and waited for Sarah to respond.

"Joe, is that you?" Sarah called out.

"No, Sadie. It's me, Mia. How are you feeling?"

"I saw my Joe while I was sleeping. I thought he was still here with me," Sarah said. She reached out her hand, signaling for Mia to come sit down beside her.

"I'm not sure how I'm feeling," Sarah replied with a raspy tone that Mia hadn't heard before. "I feel good, but then I feel bad. You seem to bring out the good, though. I'm beginning to love that about you."

Sarah's words took Mia aback. Her words were kind and gentle. They were something Mia had seen little of since she'd arrived at the nursing home. She was overwhelmed by the thought of Sarah's love. The room was dark, so Sarah couldn't see the tears forming in her eyes. Sarah might scold her for showing too much emotion.

"I keep thinking about Lucinda. I don't know how to explain it, but I feel connected to her. Like I was there, feeling what she felt and seeing what she saw."

"No need to explain things like that," Sarah said. "Just let them be. I felt the same way when she was watching me write her words. I couldn't explain it, but she became a part of me."

"What happened after you got her story? What happened to Lucinda?" Mia asked.

"Like I told you, I didn't turn her story in. I was at the school, ready to give the papers to Claudette. She was just as excited as I was. I stayed up typing those papers for days, but when the time came, fear got hold of me. Lucinda was very much alive and waiting for me to return with the news that her story was going to be told to the world. I couldn't risk her getting hurt. I couldn't bear the thought of her in pain anymore. I slipped the pages into my dress, walked out of there, and never looked back. The institute went on to publish a book of the narratives everyone collected, but I kept Lucinda's story safe with me. I regret what I did. I knew she wanted people to know the truth about what she had done and what she had lived through. I made my choice. I was even too ashamed to go back to see her."

Sarah paused, clearing her throat to allow the painful part of the memory to come forward.

"A few weeks later, Joe brought me the news that Mattie had found Lucinda's body out in the garden. Looked to be a heart attack or some other natural cause. He said Ol' Ben had lain down and died right beside her. They buried her and Ol' Ben in a cemetery somewhere, and that was that. I never told a soul about what she told me. I guess that fear didn't let me go, even after she was dead and safe. I believed I was doing the right thing, but I was wrong."

Mia could hear Sarah's voice fading in and out while she was speaking. Her words spread out, and Mia knew she had to get to the point before she lost her in the fog again.

"I have an idea that I wanted to share with you to see if you're okay with me pursuing it." Mia waited a few moments, gathering the courage to tell Sarah her idea.

"Well, go ahead and tell me, child!"

"Remember the exhibit presentation that I told you about for my job? I wanted to know if you're okay with me telling the world about Lucinda. I want to do my exhibit on you, too. I want to tell everyone about the woman who worked for the Project and gathered a first-hand account from a formerly enslaved woman named Lucinda. I want to display the pages you wrote and tell everyone about the good you and others did. I have never heard about the Works Progress Administration or the Federal Writers' Project before, and I'm sure others haven't either. I would be honored if you let me tell her story and your story, too. What do you think?"

"You mean people would know all about Lucinda in a museum?"

Mia smiled and grabbed Sarah's hand. "Yes, ma'am, they sure would!"

"That's the best idea you've had since you got here, child," Sarah softly patted Mia's hand. "That would make me very happy."

Mia was thrilled. She jumped up and hugged Sarah around the neck. "I'm going to invite you to the exhibit when it's finished, Sadie! I'm going to make sure it's amazing and well put together!"

"I couldn't ask for more." Sarah cleared her throat and reached for her glass on the nightstand. It was empty.

"I'll get some more water. Are you hungry?" Mia asked.

"A little. You can go grab us some breakfast; that would be nice." Sarah rolled back over in bed as Mia headed out of the bedroom. Just as her hand reached for the doorknob, she heard Sarah call out to her.

"Mia, I want you to know I love you. Don't you ever forget that."

Mia froze. It was as if God Himself had performed a miracle right there before her very eyes. Mia felt the tears forming once again in the corners of her eyes. That moment was what she had waited for her whole life…to be loved. Loved by her very own family. She couldn't have asked for more. She smiled and wiped the tears away as she called back out to Sarah from the doorway.

"I love you too! I really do! Would it be okay if I asked you some more questions when I get back? I have so many other things I want to ask you, Sadie. I would love to hear more stories about you and Joe.

Or what it was like writing for those newspapers for all those years. We have so much more to talk about!"

"I know by now that when Mia has questions, there isn't an option for me to say no," Sarah said. "Hurry back, and we'll talk."

Mia walked towards the cafeteria with a smile stretched from ear to ear. She couldn't remember ever being that happy. She had someone who loved her and permission now to tell the world about Lucinda. She felt as if she were floating in the clouds. The feeling was surreal.

"You're looking happy this morning," Tracy called out as Mia passed one of the residents' rooms. Mia backed up and peeked into the room to see Tracy taking someone's blood pressure.

"Sarah told me she loved me! I'm in shock!" Mia giggled.

"Wow, I guess I would be too!" Tracy stood up and patted the elderly man on the back, telling him to stop eating from his stash of saltine crackers. She wrapped up her equipment and walked out the door to meet Mia.

"You really have a positive effect on her. I see she has the same effect on you, too. You were so shy and timid when you first got here. You're more confident now and much happier!"

"If someone had told me a few days ago I would be walking around without my wig and here with my grandmother, I would've laughed at them. Being here and learning from her has been amazing! And to make things even better, I'm embracing this wild hair of mine!"

"Yeah, seeing you and that beautiful hair of yours bouncing around here these past few days has been wonderful! I should get you a permanent room here to keep her company!"

"I really do want to stay. I have to go back home to give a presentation for work; then I will be back to spend more time with her."

Tracy smiled. "That's fine with me. How's she doing this morning?"

“She’s doing okay. I could tell while we were talking that she was going in and out, so I’m grabbing her some breakfast, and then we can spend the day together.”

“That’s perfect. Go grab her some food, and I’ll go in and give her the medications she needs to take for the morning.”

Mia and Tracy parted ways as Mia made her way to the cafeteria. She floated from table to table, grabbing all of Sarah’s favorite foods, including oranges. She didn’t have a care in the world at that moment, and she held on tight to the happiness surrounding her.

Standing at the coffee table, she watched two nurses run into the cafeteria, signaling for others to follow. Mia couldn’t make out what they were saying, but she could tell it was important. She grabbed her tray, making her way back to Sarah’s room. Mia hadn’t walked far before a jolt of fear ran up her back as she saw that the nurses who ran into the cafeteria were now coming in and out of Sarah’s doorway. Mia dropped the tray on the floor and ran into the room to see what was going on. Tracy was coming out and caught sight of Mia rushing down the hall. She grabbed her by the shoulders, pulling her away from the room.

“What’s going on, Tracy? Why won’t you let me in? Where’s Sarah?”

“Mia, calm down, please calm down,” Tracy begged. Mia screamed for Tracy to let go of her, but Tracy grabbed Mia close, holding on to her shaking body.

“Mia, listen to me.” Mia could see tears forming in the folds of Tracy’s eyes. The happiness that covered her heart was now gone, and Mia felt anxiety taking form. She watched as the nurses left the room, making phone calls for the paramedics to come.

“Mia, she wasn’t responsive when I came in to give her medication. They are in there now, doing CPR and using the defibrillator. We’re waiting for the paramedics to come. They’re on the way.”

"But...but...I was just in there with her. She was fine. She told me she loved me, and she was fine. Let me see her. Let me see her!" Tracy held onto Mia tightly as she screamed and clawed for the door. Mia could feel her heart racing. Soon, the room grew a dark shade of muted black. Tracy could feel Mia's breathing getting heavy as she pressed against her chest.

"Mia!" Tracy screamed. Mia's vision went dark, and she fell to the floor as the four black walls closed in on her.

CHAPTER THIRTY-SEVEN

REMEMBER

Mia came to, blurry-eyed and rattled, trying to remember where she was and how she got there. She focused her eyes on a figure sitting beside her and tried to make out who it was. She cleared her throat and sat up from the table she was lying on. Her body felt stiff.

"Take it easy, Mia," the blurry figure whispered. "You passed out a little while ago, and you need to lie down."

Mia rubbed her eyes as she saw Scott come into focus. The only thing that Mia could think about or even care to know was where Sarah was and if she was okay. Mia looked around the room, searching for a sign of Sarah.

"Where is she?" Mia tearfully demanded. Her voice cracked as she pushed Scott's hands away from her. "Where is Sarah? Is she okay?"

"I can tell you soon, but first, you need to—"

Mia slammed her hand down on the table, demanding again to be told where Sarah was. Scott could see Mia would not do what he asked, nor would she stop until she received news of Sarah's condition. Scott backed out of the room and called out for Tracy to come help. Mia covered her face with her shaking palms and cried. Tracy soon slipped into the room and stood next to Mia. She gently placed her hands on Mia's and eased them down from her face.

"Mia," Tracy whispered with heavy remorse. "I'm so sorry, Mia. Sarah passed away. There was nothing more we could've done. The paramedics took her to the funeral home. I'm so sorry."

Mia lay back down on the table and turned her back to Tracy, asking to be left alone. Tracy nodded her head, leaving Mia in the room by herself. She burst into tears, screaming and banging her fist against the thick plastered wall beside her. She stayed that way for hours, banging and crying, screaming and shaking. There was nothing she could do or say to bring Sarah back. No amount of tears that ran from her eyes could drown out her pain.

Mia emerged from the small nurse's station a few hours later, still shaking. Tracy was sitting by the door the entire time, keeping close to Mia to ensure she didn't have another anxiety attack. After hearing Mia's screams, she wasn't sure what could happen. Tracy watched as Mia inched her way down the corridor, dragging her feet with each step. All the life had drained from her. She was in a clear state of shock. She stared blankly ahead, with nothing to say or feel.

Tracy quietly followed Mia as she headed to Sarah's room. Mia gently opened the door as the familiar scent of fresh mint once again filled her senses. She paused in the doorway, taking deep breaths of the crisp air, focusing on the eclectic array of items still scattered around the room. The tears welled in the corner of her eyes as her focus centered on Sarah's bedroom door. She hoped Sarah would come rolling out in her wheelchair, telling her to move or to shut up. Every item in the room remained intact, but the space was lifeless without Sarah to give it purpose.

Sarah was gone. Mia sat down at the kitchen table and grabbed an apple from the fruit bowl. Tracy sat at the table with her, remaining silent. She could see that Mia was still in shock. Mia took a few bites and muttered to Tracy.

"I'm sorry if I was mean to you, Tracy."

"You've nothing to be sorry for, Mia. I understand Sarah meant a lot to you."

"What are you going to do with all of her things?"

"Well, we normally donate items that are unclaimed by family members. You're more than welcome to take whatever items you want."

"Thank you."

"Mia…there's something else that I need to tell you. Now that Sarah's gone, I'm responsible for ensuring her estate is handled properly, but if you need time, I understand. We can talk later. I know this may not be the best time to discuss these types of matters."

"No. You can tell me now," Mia said. "I won't be more prepared to talk later than I am now. What do you have to tell me?"

"Well, David wasn't being entirely honest when he told everyone that he didn't have any money left. When Sarah came to live here, he asked me if I would be a trustee over an account he had set up for her. He wanted to make sure that if she ever needed anything, she was taken care of. On the account, David named Sarah the primary beneficiary. He wasn't sure he would ever have kids when he set it up, so he listed "Next of Kin" as the contingent beneficiary. That would've been Valerie, that is, until you came along."

"What does that mean for me?"

"Mr. Lucas is entrusted to handle all the legal paperwork, but that would mean that you are to inherit the funds in the account."

"I'm pretty sure Sarah spent that money already. Look at all of this stuff in here. She had to have spent a fortune on these things."

"No." Tracy smiled at her. "She had these things before she got here. David told her about the account when she arrived, but I believe after years of not needing much and the memory loss her condition caused, she just forgot that the money was there to spend."

"How much did he leave her?" Mia asked.

"He left her around $15,000. She never touched it, so all the funds are still there."

"You mean…you mean…the money belongs to me?"

"Yes, it does. I spoke with Mr. Lucas while you were in the nurse's office. He wants to discuss Sarah's funeral arrangements with you as well as Sarah's estate. He will be contacting you soon."

"But…I…$15,000?" Mia was speechless. She couldn't believe what Tracy had told her. Tracy leaned over and rubbed the tears from Mia's face.

"I'll give you some time alone, Mia." She stood up from the table and walked out of the room.

Mia didn't know what to do or say. Her body felt uneasy. She needed to lie down. She stood up from the table and walked into Sarah's bedroom. Mia sank into the cold sheets of Sarah's bed and breathed deeply into the pillows, taking in Sarah's lingering scent. It suddenly occurred to her that during her time with Sarah, Sarah had never turned on the lights in her bedroom. Mia reached to turn on the lamp, filling the small room with light. She looked around the room for a moment, then something caught her eye. There behind the door were several index cards, taped up on the wall and covered in scribbled sentences. Mia walked over to get a closer look at what was written on the cards. She pulled a few from the wall and read them aloud.

"His name is David. He is your son. You love him."

Other cards read, *"You love to write, and you are very good at it."*

"You are from Norfolk, Virginia."

"You don't like Evelyn, and you don't like Gwendolyn. They hog the TV."

"Valerie is the devil!"

Mia continued reading the cards one by one. She soon realized why the cards were there. Sarah must've put them there to help her remember what she was slowly forgetting. Mia remembered Sarah's need to keep the lights off in her room. It pained her to think of Sarah being ashamed to have the cards up and being embarrassed about her condition. Mia came to the last card on the wall and pulled it off.

"Her name is Mia. She is your granddaughter. Always remember that she is beautiful and you love her."

CHAPTER THIRTY-EIGHT

FORGIVENESS

Silence. The silence made the darkness unbearable.

It was there in the darkness where Mia wanted to remain. She was home now. She wasn't sure if she wanted to call it home anymore. Home felt like love. Home was where Sarah was. There was nothing left for her to love now that Sarah was gone.

She shut out the world, keeping her door locked and her windows shut. She aimlessly paced the floor, searching for something that wasn't there. Exhausted but too anxious to sleep, occasionally, she pulled back the curtains to stare off into the distance and place her thoughts on the busy streets outside her windows. *Everyone is moving and living their life—everyone except me.*

At other times, she stopped pacing and took a moment to admire the items she was able to bring back from Sarah's room. She had packed her car tight, not wanting to leave anything behind. Even though Tracy promised to mail what she couldn't take back, she still felt horrible about leaving anything there. Standing over one of Sarah's beautiful ceramic vases, she rubbed its glazed exterior and felt the rigid grooves and lines of the raised acrylic paint on her grandfather's artwork. Mia remembered how much Sarah loved and hated the paintings that he had made for her. She lifted the pots of fresh mint to breathe in their fragrance and remember how Sarah loved to chew on the stems. Sarah's knick-knacks, blankets, and other items were also scattered around the room. The most prized possessions she removed were the large gray tote, full of pictures from Sarah's past, and the shoebox that held the yellowed pages of Lucinda's life. Mia wanted so badly to look inside the tote. There were so many things from Sarah's past that sat within reach, but Mia couldn't find the courage to look at them.

Mia and her depression sat together quietly in the apartment. It was almost time for her to present her exhibit idea to Mr. Garner, but she didn't have a single word prepared. She didn't care. Nothing mattered to her anymore. Not work, not her friendship with Bee, not even the money Sarah had left behind.

Bee called and came by several times, trying to contact Mia. The only time Bee got an answer out of Mia was when she slid a note under Mia's door. Mia wrote, *Sarah died. I just want to be left alone right now* and pushed it back under the door for Bee to read and leave. Although she succeeded in ignoring most everyone in her life, there was one person who she could not escape.

While deep into one of her usual slow walks around the apartment, Mia was startled by a loud knock at the door. It was a knock she knew all too well. She cringed, knowing that her unwelcome visitor would not stop banging without her opening the door. She dragged herself over to look through the peephole and flung her head back with a sigh of disgust.

"Mia Renee Briggs!" yelled Norma. "You open this door right now, or else I'm going to kick it down! Open it now!"

Mia pressed her back against the door. There was no one on earth she wanted to see less than Norma.

"Norma, I'm fine. I just want to be left alone." Mia shouted through the thick metal door.

"I said open this door, Mia!"

Norma continued shouting and banging on the door. Mia surrendered her fight, unhooked the latch, and opened the door. She walked back towards the couch, knowing Norma would be following close behind. Norma came barging in, slamming the door behind her. Mia calmly sat down on the couch, paying no attention to her mother.

"It stinks in here, Mia. Why do you have all the lights off? What's going on with you? Why haven't you returned any of my calls?" Norma continued on, question after question, and Mia became more irritated with every word that came out of her mouth.

"Last time I checked, *Mom*, I don't have to—"

"Don't you get sassy with me, young lady! I have no problem with whoopin' your ass!"

"Why are you here?" Mia yelled. "What do you want? I don't understand why you keep bothering me when all I want to do is to be left alone!" Mia felt the tears build up in her eyes. She pressed her hands to her face and began to cry.

Norma stood there with her hand still balled up. She immediately noticed what was going on with Mia. She could see by the look of Mia's apartment, and the smell coming from it, too, that Mia needed help. Norma had never seen Mia that way. She knew her daughter was a bit messy and unorganized at times, but what she saw before her went way beyond that. There were dirty dishes piled up in the sink. Dirty clothes flung over chairs and the couch. Old food and trash littered around the kitchen and into the living room.

Norma loved Mia. If there was ever a time she could prove that, it was now. She could smell the stench of depression in the air. She knew that smell all too well. It was pungent, filling her with fatigue on restless nights when her parents' memories refused to recede. It was the odor that lingered after David left for Virginia, and the day she and David were reunited, it saturated the air once again with the grave epiphany that he was dying. It had been hard to live with that constant, dismal smell. Empathy filled her heart as she walked over to the couch and sat beside Mia.

"I want to know what's going on, Mia," Norma said slowly. "You haven't answered my calls or any of my messages. I reached out to Elizabeth to see if she had spoken with you. She told me what happened with Sarah. I'm so sorry to hear she passed away. I know not having a family has been hard on you, so losing Sarah is very difficult, but you can't shut everyone out."

"I would've known about her sooner if you weren't so selfish," Mia said as she sniffled, trying to talk through her tears. "All I have are her things here with me. That's it. That's all I have left to remember her by."

Norma sat beside her, not making a sound. She wanted to give Mia time to work through her emotions. Mia went on rambling, trying to make sense of it all. She didn't even notice Norma trying to comfort her at first, but then it hit her that her mother was being…nice. Mia peeked through her fingers to confirm she hadn't gone completely crazy. It was definitely Norma rubbing her back. Norma noticed Mia looking over at her in disbelief and withdrew her hand.

"Mia, I want you to know that I understand how painful this is for you. I'm not going to lie to you and say that I didn't go through the same thing when I found out how my real parents died. Even when I got the news that David died. He was the only man I ever loved, and even though we were apart for so long, I still love him to this very day."

"That doesn't help me at all. No matter what you say, he is still gone. Sarah is still gone."

"Mia, since you left, I've been thinking, and I need to be honest with you about all of this. I realized all your pain and missing precious time with David and Sarah could have been prevented. I…I didn't know how to tell you about your father's family every time you asked. Even though David agreed to keep everything a secret, I should've told you the truth from the beginning. Honestly, part of me was jealous, and I truly believed that I was all you needed and would ever need. I raised you by myself, and I assumed that was enough. I thought sheltering you would keep you safe. I thought requiring excellence from you would make you love me, but I was so wrong. I heard the happiness in your voice briefly when I called you. I knew it was because you finally got the answers you always wanted. Then I heard that same happiness fade away as soon as you heard it was me on the other end. We've yelled at each other so many times, but in that moment, I finally heard how much you hated me and how much I've hurt you. Trust me, I hate myself for what I've done to you. There's no way to bring David or Sarah back, but Mia, you can't go on like this. You have to be strong not only for yourself, but for them. What would Sarah say if she saw you like this?"

Mia paused for a moment in disbelief. Norma's confession startled her, and she looked at her mother in shock. *Did she just apologize?* Then she remembered the side of Sarah that she first met and how Sarah would have cursed her out, seeing her that way. Mia hadn't thought about it that way, how Sarah would react if she saw her having a pity party. Then she remembered what Sarah had told her: "Forgive your mother." Forgiving Norma would mean accepting the lies and embracing the pain, but how could she forgive Norma when she was the reason she'd missed the opportunity to be with David and Sarah? As badly as she wanted to dismiss Sarah's words, they continued to echo in her mind.

She thought about Lucinda and the horrible things she had seen and faced, things she never told Sarah about. The pain she must've felt time and time again, all while continuing on and not giving up on herself. Lucinda kept going. Sarah kept going. She remembered Lucinda's words: "It is well." Both women lost more than Mia could ever imagine losing. She decided at that moment that she'd do her best to keep going too.

"Thank you, Mom. I needed to hear that." Mia smiled.

"I know. I remember what you said about therapy and us going together. I think after all this, it would be a good idea. I'm willing to try if you are."

Mia stood up and did something she'd never done before. She wrapped her arms around her mother and hugged her as tight as she could. Norma was shocked by Mia's abrupt movement into her once-guarded space, but she didn't fight the moment. She wrapped her arms around Mia too, and the two stood there in an unexpected embrace. Norma kissed Mia on the forehead and sent her to her room to rest. She stayed in the apartment, cleaning and making dinner. Norma did everything she could to help her daughter return to a state of normalcy. For once in her life, she was acting like the mother Mia truly needed.

CHAPTER THIRTY-NINE

CHOSEN

"That concludes my presentation. Thank you." Mia nervously looked around the room for reactions.

Mr. Garner stood up from his chair at the end of the long meeting table. His eyes were fixed on her, and Mia braced herself for impact. She was sure that he could see how nervous she was. Mia had scrambled the night before to assemble a worthwhile presentation for Mr. Garner and the rest of the museum staff. She pieced together visual slides from documents she pulled on the Federal Writers' Project under the then-titled Works Progress Administration. She spoke about the incredible work that had been done and stood proud as she revealed the yellowed pages of Lucinda's story to the room. Bee, who was standing in the corner of the room, smiled, happy to see her best friend again.

"Mia Briggs…that was absolutely fantastic!" Mr. Garner began clapping wildly. "What an idea! I'll let you slide on the lack of preparation, as you know I normally require folders for everyone to review. However, I know you've been through a lot recently, but overall, this is the best idea I've heard all day!"

"Thank you, Mr. Garner." Mia was in total shock that he enjoyed her idea.

"This is the type of unsaturated history we need to display! You even have an original typed narrative."

Mr. Garner walked over to Mia and patted her on the back. "Mia, your presentation will be the main exhibit for the grand opening!" Mr. Garner called Yvonne over to him and gave her instructions.

"Yvonne, I will send you a list of contacts to see who's willing to loan us artifacts for the exhibit. Let me check my contacts, I have at the historical society out in the Tidewater area. I need to see what they can dig up for us, too." Mr. Garner continued instructing everyone in the room. He assigned everyone something to work on to begin creating Mia's exhibit.

Mia wanted to be thrilled, too. She wanted to jump up and down with joy. She wanted to be happy, and even more grateful, that she still had a job after all that time spent with Sarah. Bee walked over to Mia after Mr. Garner and the rest of the staff left the meeting room, pulled out a chair, and signaled for Mia to sit down.

"You missed my birthday."

"I know, and I know saying 'I'm sorry' isn't going to fix how I've treated you."

"I'm just glad to see you out of your apartment, Mia."

"Bee, I really do want to say I'm sorry. I've been treating you so badly and ignoring you when all you were trying to do was make sure I was okay. You've been nothing but good to me."

"You don't have to apologize, Mia. I know how happy you were to have Sarah. You were finally with your family. I can't imagine how good that must have felt. So, I totally get that you're hurt."

The two quickly caught each other up on what was going on in their lives, with Bee having so much to tell Mia about since she left. Mia sat back, indulging in Bee's conversation. She missed her friend and was relieved that she hadn't given up on her.

"How are you doing, though? I mean, how are you *really* doing?" asked Bee.

"I've been trying to get out of this funk," Mia replied. "I even let Norma come into my apartment and help me clean up."

"Norma? You let your mom in your house?!"

"Yes, she's been cleaning and cooking for me. We've been talking too. She's acting like a totally different person."

"Maybe she saw how down you were and decided to have some compassion for once."

"Yeah, I guess. It's been a lot to deal with. I'm afraid to think of what's next." Mia sighed.

"Maybe this is the start of something great for you, Mia!" Bee proclaimed. "You have the floor for the main exhibit of the grand opening now. Did you see Camille's face when Mr. Garner started clapping? I know she was sure she had the spot with that exhibit idea about the history of voodoo and witchcraft in the South. Now, who wants to bring their family to see all that?"

Mia chuckled. It was the first time she'd smiled in days.

"There's something else that happened."

"What? Is everything okay?" Bee reached over and placed her hand on Mia's shoulder.

"Yes, everything's fine. I got news that Sarah had an account left to her by my dad."

"An account! Oh, my God! Does that mean you're rich?!"

"No," said Mia. "I'm not rich, but I did get some money. He left her $15,000 and—"

Bee jumped out of her seat. "Mia, you're rich! Do you know how many wigs $15,000 could buy you?!"

"Yeah, a lot, but I'm done with wigs. Sarah taught me how beautiful I am without them. I feel better without them anyway." Bee smiled and grabbed Mia in a loving embrace.

"I was wondering what caused you not to have one on today. I thought you were still depressed and had forgotten. I hated those wigs anyway. I'm so proud of you! You're so beautiful, Mia. So, what are you going to do with all that money then?"

"I don't know yet. I need to get my car fixed, but I have no idea what to do with the rest. Sarah's funeral is in a few days. I want to make sure everything's perfect for her."

"Did you tell Norma about the money?"

"No way! She would try to tell me what to do with it. I'm going to spend this money how I want to spend it."

"Well, it will come to you, and if you want to send your best friend some of it, she won't be mad!" Bee said as she nudged Mia.

Mia stood up and walked to the office door. She locked arms with Bee as she opened the door.

"Will you help me work on this project? I need you right by my side."

"Of course!" said Bee. "I wouldn't have it any other way."

CHAPTER FORTY

EPIPHANY

Norma's presence and change of heart helped pull Mia out of her depressed state, little by little. Days passed, and she became a little more focused and a little more conscious of her personal hygiene every day. Bee frequently stopped by to help Mia with her exhibit. Mia was glad to have Bee by her side again as the two friends once again sat on Mia's couch, talking and laughing. They paid no attention to Norma, who was cooking lunch in the kitchen and eavesdropping on their conversation.

There was a knock at the door. Norma wiped her flour-covered hands on a dish towel and went to answer the door. Mia looked up from the couch to see Yvonne standing at the door with a folder in her hand.

"Hi, Yvonne!" Mia jumped up from the couch and made her way to the door. "What brings you here?"

"Hello, Mia. Mr. Garner insisted that I bring you this folder today. A friend of his down in Tidewater found some pictures in an archive. Mr. Garner wanted you to see them right away."

"Well, thank you. You came all this way to drop these off? You're so sweet."

"Actually, I never realized how close we live to each other. I'm only two blocks away, so it was no trouble at all. Well, go ahead and open it. I'm excited to see what he found, too!"

Mia carefully slid her fingernail under the crease of the folder and pulled the flap open. She first pulled out a single black-and-white photo, blown up so the people in it were visible. Mia inspected the photo. There was a young white woman, seated in a chair, dressed in a silk, Victorian-style dress with curls throughout her hair. She looked as if she were dressed to go to a party. To her side stood a young black woman, wearing a patterned cotton dress with a scarf twisted around her head. Mia looked at the picture a few times.

"Who are they?" she asked.

"I would tell you to guess, but I'm pretty sure you aren't in the mood for guessing games," Yvonne replied. "Remember, at the exhibit presentation meeting, how you told everyone about Lucinda and the woman who took her in, named Mary? Well, Mr. Garner's friend down at the historical society did some digging to see if we could find any pictures of Lucinda. They couldn't find any of her at first, so then they tried Mary Brock, and that's when they got a hit! Historical documents stated that Mary was invited to a dinner in honor of her late husband. They took a picture of her at the event and published it in the newspaper. Apparently, she had Lucinda right by her side and refused to take the picture without her."

"You mean…that's…that's Lucinda?" squeaked Mia.

"Yep! Sure is! I know it's kind of hard to see, but there's the scar on her leg you talked about! The historical society agreed to let us use the original for the exhibit. Everyone has been helping out, making sure that your exhibit is a success! He wanted to be the first one to tell you about what they found, but I suggested that I come instead since I live nearby."

Mia stood frozen, holding the photo in her hand, staring at the woman in the picture. While reading the yellowed pages with Sarah, Mia had formed her own idea of how Lucinda looked. She imagined her to have a strong face, beautiful eyes, and a slender frame. She made up someone in her mind that she could reach for when she needed her, and there she was. Mia no longer had to imagine. Lucinda was more beautiful than she could have ever imagined. Mia covered her mouth, still shocked. She smiled and reached over to hug Yvonne.

"This is amazing, Yvonne! Thank you so much. I can't begin to tell you what this means to me!"

"Oh! There's one other thing," said Yvonne. "Mr. Garner looked up the name you mentioned in the meeting. Umm…Nitakupata. I thought it was a lovely name myself, but we researched it, and it turns out it's not a name but a phrase."

Yvonne took the folder from Mia and reached to the bottom, pulling out a piece of paper with notes scribbled on the front.

"Here it is. We found out it actually means *I will find you* in Swahili."

Mia's heart sank to the floor. *I will find you*. It broke her to know those were the last words Lucinda's mother left her with. To know the pain she must've felt to die without finding her. Having to cut into her baby that way, and Lucinda having to do the same to her daughter.

Before she could respond, Norma nudged herself from behind the door and looked at the photo Mia was holding. She noticed something in the photo. She looked at the bottom of Lucinda's leg, focusing on the clear and visible scar.

"I've seen that scar before," Norma whispered.

"What? Are you okay, Norma?" Mia asked.

"Mia, I've seen that scar before," repeated Norma. She grabbed the photo from Mia's hands and sprinted into Mia's room. Norma emerged, dragging the large tote from the bedroom.

"What are you doing, Norma?" cried Mia. "Why are you opening Sarah's box?"

"I know you are going to get upset, but while you were at work, I went into it. I looked at all the photos that were in here."

"You did what? How could you!" Mia yelled. "That box is private. You didn't have any right to open it!"

"Mia, hush for one minute. I'm sorry I invaded your privacy but listen to me! I'm trying to tell you I saw that same scar on someone in this box!"

Norma, unsure of what she had stumbled upon, began digging wildly through the heavy tote. Pictures flew in every direction. Finally, she came to the shoe box that belonged to Sarah's mother. She opened it and retrieved the photo she'd been looking for. She called Mia over, putting the two images together so she could see them.

"Do you see it? I'm not crazy, am I?" Mia took the photos from Norma, reluctant to answer the latter question. She stared at them and saw what Norma meant. She looked at the albumen-printed photo of a well-dressed black woman holding a baby boy on her hip and a small girl standing beside her. There on the woman's leg was the same scar Lucinda had.

These past few days, Mia hadn't touched the tote. She did not want to look at the photos for fear of seeing David or Sarah and feeling more depressed than she already was. The only photos she'd seen from the tote were the ones that she'd seen with Sarah at the kitchen table.

"Bee," called Mia. "Tell me you see what I see, too." Bee walked over and examined the photo.

"I do. I do, but what does this mean? Who's this woman?"

Mia flipped the photo over to reveal the inscription: "Hannah, child Ruth and child Martin." Mia wasn't sure of what she had stumbled upon either. She began pacing around the room, holding the two photos in her hands, talking to herself and trying to make sense of what she was looking at.

Sarah said that her mother's name was Ruth. I'm sure of it. She said she had never met her grandmother because she'd died before she was born. If this is Ruth in the photo, then that's Ruth's mother in there with her. Hannah. Sarah never said her name, I think. But Hannah has the same scar as Lucinda. Lucinda put a scar, identical to hers, on her daughter before she was sold away. If this woman, Hannah, has the same scar as Lucinda, then that must mean she's—

"Oh my God!" Mia screamed, jumping up and down. "It's…I think…I think!"

"Mia! Mia!" yelled Bee. "Calm down! What's going on? Who is that?"

"It's her!" Mia loudly proclaimed. "It's Lucinda's daughter, her Little One!" Bee looked at Mia with confusion as Mia recited everything she had put together in her mind.

"Wait a minute, wait a minute, Mia," Bee waved her hand for Mia to listen to her. "I thought you said Sarah saw Lucinda's scar. How could she not match Hannah's scar with Lucinda's? Weren't these Sarah's photos?" Mia paused, then remembered what Sarah had said about the photos.

"Sarah said she never looked at these photos because she didn't like looking at dead people. Her mom died before she met Lucinda. There was no way for her to put two and two together if her mom never told her about the scar and she never saw a photo of her grandmother."

Bee realized there might be some truth to what Mia was saying. Mia sat back down on the couch. She looked deep into Lucinda's eyes.

Norma walked over to Mia and sat beside her on the couch. She, too, began to recite the facts aloud to piece the puzzle together.

"Mia, do you realize what that means? If Sarah is Ruth's daughter, and Ruth is Hannah's daughter, and Hannah is Lucinda's daughter, then..."

"Mia, that means you're related to Lucinda!" yelled Bee. "You're like her great-great-great-granddaughter or something!" Bee nudged Mia, excited about the fascinating discovery.

Mia was stuck in a state of shock.

She excused herself from the room, walked to the bathroom, and shut the door behind her. She needed a moment alone to process what was happening.

Everything had come full circle. She was speechless at the thought that Lucinda's blood could flow through her own veins, but ultimately heartbroken that the truth could never be confirmed. Mia knew that was the drawback of history, but at that moment, she chose to believe the impossible. She chose to believe that the random events were not random at all, but were intricately planned by fate. Mia stood in front of the bathroom mirror, staring into her reflection. To know that Lucinda's prayers were answered was more than she ever could've asked for. It was by fate that Sarah found Lucinda, and without realizing it, the two shared a deeper bond than either one had known.

It wasn't just Lucinda that Mia found in those worn and yellowed pages, but she found herself, too. She could hear the words Lucinda gave to Sarah, now filling every part of her. She felt comforted by a sense of peace from all the events that had brought her to that exact moment. There was no hurt, no bitterness, and no darkness. She could feel the walls built up in her mind begin to crumble and fall beneath her feet. She ran her fingers through her hair and smiled. No longer would she feel ashamed of the strands of hair that bounced all around her head. All the strength and beauty she hadn't realized was there now looked back at her proudly from the other side of the mirror. She had found herself, just as Lucinda would have wanted.

She wanted nothing else at that moment but to allow forgiveness in. Sarah had taught Mia the weight of forgiveness. Forgiveness that forced her to relinquish her right to anger. Forgiveness that was once painful but had ultimately become a freeing decision to choose peace, even though her pain still had a voice. She forgave David for his careless actions. She forgave Sarah for her regrettable decision. She forgave Lucinda, washing away the blood of her slave master from her hands. She forgave Norma and her broken heart. She forgave herself for allowing her fears to bring her to the point of darkness, a place where she had once been a prisoner. It was forgiveness that each of them sought, and forgiveness was found.

CHAPTER FORTY-ONE

FOUND

Mia could still feel the beaded raindrops clinging to her thin jacket. The cold chill in the air pressed into her skin, sending a shudder through her tense body. She looked out over the dampened headstones that lined the graveyard. The tree branches hung low, pressed down by the weight of the rain. Her pain became stronger, knowing she would have to leave Sarah in that cold, lifeless place. She recalled the words the preacher spoke that echoed across the cemetery; words meant to comfort the pain and somehow meant to comfort her, too. Sitting in the front row, she watched strangers lay their budding roses on top of the casket. Each walked by to offer their condolences to Mia. She could still taste the salt-filled tears that fell, getting tangled in the raindrops that ran alongside them.

Mia watched Tracy and the others from the nursing home gather around, crying collective tears for Sarah. Evelyn was even there, stone-faced and saddened by the turn of events that took Sarah away. The scent of fresh lilies and carnations permeated the air. They cascaded over the casket and podium, giving life a chance among death. She did her best to make sure everything was perfect, right down to the absence of Valerie.

As the preacher reached out to signal that the casket be closed, Mia stood and asked if she could see Sarah one more time. Bee, sitting next to Mia, reached over to confirm this was what she wanted to do. Mia nodded her head with assurance, and the preacher agreed. Her fear of death had subsided. She was stronger now. She took one last look at Sarah's still face. She had made sure that Sarah's long, beautiful gray hair was pinned up and proper, just the way her mother, Ruth, would've wanted. Sarah's makeup was soft and tasteful. Mia requested she be dressed in a brand new pink floral muumuu with a matching pair of pink bedroom slippers. She knew it's what Sarah would've wanted. Mia leaned in and placed a picture of Sarah and David into the creases of the silk lining. She then pulled a copy of the picture of Lucinda from her pocket and laid it in with Sarah, too. She leaned over and kissed Sarah's cold forehead. *"I love you, Sadie,"* she whispered and took a few steps back as a pallbearer closed the casket.

Mia felt a hand pressing into her shoulder. She looked up to find herself where she had been, sitting in the corner of the room where the exhibit was already taking place. She wiped the tears from her eyes and tucked her last memory of Sarah safely away.

"Mia, are you okay?" Norma patted Mia's back. "It's almost time for you to give your speech."

"Yeah, I'm okay. Thanks again for helping me with everything, Mom."

"No, baby, thank you for giving me a chance to make things up to you. Besides that, our therapist has been keeping me in check these last few weeks! She let me know I have a lot of work to do, but she is right about one thing: we're making progress, and I couldn't be prouder of you, Mia. This exhibit is beyond anything I could have imagined!"

Norma kissed Mia on the forehead and playfully fluffed her thick head of curls. "You look fantastic! These curls of yours have really grown on me! Good luck with your speech, baby. I'll be right over there if you need me." Norma straightened the collar of Mia's blouse and made her way back into the crowd.

Mia looked around the room, filled with colorful balloons and streamers celebrating the grand opening. The place was bustling with people everywhere. She was pleasantly surprised that everyone had braved the cold February morning, trudging through the snow. Friends and strangers were scattered throughout, admiring the finished project. She had paid little attention to anyone entering the exhibit hall, too caught up in the moment, recalling the day she had to say goodbye to Sarah. A gentle smile played on her lips as she took in the lively room full of friends and guests. Tracy was there too, standing beside one of the displays with Bee by her side, both reading its description with interest.

Mia rose and headed for the stage, browsing the exhibit, feeling a sense of pride that her vision had materialized, highlighting the Federal Writers' Project's impactful work for the community. Over several weeks, she studied various facets of the Federal Writers' Project, including the Virginia Negro Studies Project. She spent several hours at the library exploring the Library of Congress's online Slave Narrative Collection, containing thousands of pages of stories recorded by contracted field workers, including Sarah and Claudette. She gazed into the large shadow boxes lining the walls, each containing delicate artifacts from the past. The forgotten words of formerly enslaved people were displayed. Copies of invaluable books such as *These Are Our Lives*, *Lay My Burden Down* and *The Negro in Virginia*, which were products of the Project, were provided for visitors to look through. Glass cases held sheets of vibrant songs and hymns sung by enslaved people. Alongside them were the makeshift instruments used to bring joy to dark times.

Among the artifacts were life-sized photos of those who had shared their stories. Pictures of brave men and women who had survived the unthinkable. The black-and-white photos were life-sized so visitors could get a clear glimpse into their eyes. Lost stories were in those eyes. Some men still had the scars from cotton thorns deep in their hands. Women with full lips, their backs riddled with scars, yet still able to stand strong. Mia stopped at one of the women's photos. She stood tall and proud, with a thick headwrap on top of her head. She gazed into the woman's eyes and smiled. It was as if Lucinda were there with her, giving her the strength she needed. She kissed the tips of her fingers and pressed her hand on Lucinda's cheek.

"Ladies and gentlemen," Mr. Garner announced, "I would like to introduce to you the visionary of this fascinating exhibit. She's an asset to this museum, and I would love for her to talk about her vision and how the idea of paying homage to those who have gone before us came to be. Ladies and gentlemen, Mia Briggs!" Everyone in the audience clapped and cheered for Mia. She took her place in front of the microphone and waited for the crowd to settle.

"Thank you all for being here today. It means so much to me that you came to celebrate with us on a snowy day like this. This exhibit wasn't something that immediately came to me. I had to meet and lose someone dear to me for all of this to come to life. The exhibits and displays before you are of special importance because they are firsthand accounts of our ancestors. Those who lived before us and fought for the freedoms we enjoy today. This exhibit means more to me than anyone could understand. Before all of this, I didn't understand what my heritage and race meant. Being a black woman was just something I was born into. Then I met my grandmother, Sarah Newell. She was a decorated journalist who dedicated her life to making sure that everyone's truth was told. She lived through the Great Depression and worked alongside others in the Virginia Negro Studies Project, a subset of the Federal Writers' Project under FDR's Works Progress Administration. As fate would have it, she

collected only one narrative from a woman named Lucinda, whom I now believe to be her great-grandmother. Although my grandmother didn't know it at the time, I believe that she knows now. Their stories live within me, and I'm proud to now share them with the world.

"Today, you'll see dozens of stories, artifacts, and other pieces of history, all dedicated to telling the truths of formerly enslaved people. Some may be hard to read; others may make you smile. What you won't see today is my story. My story of being lost and afraid. That is, until I met Sarah and Lucinda. They opened my eyes so quickly and turned my world upside down. What you won't see in this exhibit is what I've taken away from this. Knowing that the blood of my ancestors, Lucinda and Sarah, runs through my veins. Their stories, strength, and wisdom will carry me every day. What you won't see are the changes that have occurred within me. I now realize the beauty I once overlooked in things like my hair. I used to hate my hair because other people made fun of how it looked. Then I learned along this journey that my great-great-great-grandmother was forced to have her head shaved, all because her beauty was too much for someone else to see. But the most freeing part of all of this is what both Lucinda and Sarah have taught me about forgiveness. They both went through life looking for absolution for their actions but never fully received a release from their guilt. The weight of forgiveness can be heavy, but the reward of peace is well worth it. I've learned that forgiveness is for me and done through me and not the person who wronged me. I am free now because I chose to forgive. These changes help me every day to release my fears, doubts, and anxiety, knowing that Lucinda told me that it is well.

"To my surprise, after my grandmother's passing, I was made aware that she left behind a significant amount of money that now belonged to me. For months, I was unsure of what to do with it. Then, a few weeks ago, I had a dream of standing beside a stream. I could feel the cold air coming from the water. I was barefoot and could feel the grass between

my toes. It felt so real. Then I saw my grandmother, Sarah, standing beside me, and Lucinda nearby. I saw it in her eyes that night that she was grateful that I had found our family and that I was going to tell their stories.

"After careful consideration, I've decided to contribute the money to making this exhibit a permanent part of our museum. From this day forward, I want everyone who lays eyes on these amazing individuals and who reads their stories to know the truth, their truth, no matter how harsh or somber it may be. This exhibit area is now dedicated as the Nitakupata Exhibit Hall, because I hope that among these faces and stories, you'll one day find yourself, just as I've found myself and my family. Thank you."

AUTHOR'S NOTE

This novel began as a college homework assignment.

We were tasked with further researching the classroom discussion topic, which centered on the Works Progress Administration (WPA), later renamed the Work Projects Administration. Before that day, I had never been introduced to the Federal Writers' Project under the WPA or to the many amazing projects it completed during its active years. I'm not sure if knowing about what I learned that day would have sparked this story sooner, but I know that when I heard of it, Mia, Sarah, and Lucinda appeared in my view. I saw three generations of women, all affected somehow by this fascinating project created during the Great Depression. That homework assignment turned into a short story, with several (and I mean several) different plot twists and other characters. That then became a four-year journey of studying historical facts, reading the narratives of formerly enslaved individuals, and more.

One of my primary sources was the ***Born in Slavery: Slave Narratives from the Federal Writers' Project, 1936–1938*** collection, which has over 2,300 first-person accounts and 500 photographs of enslaved people from the Library of Congress[1]. The narratives collected were real and raw. Some narratives I read spoke of pleasant experiences with their slave masters, while others depicted horrible moments in time that required me to put down the manuscript for a while to gather my thoughts. I also learned of the controversies surrounding the administration, including racial tensions and shifting priorities, such as funding World War II. I ultimately omitted this historical element from the book.

Lucinda's dialogue is also captured in the same way that would have been recorded by one of the Federal field workers at that time. Their instructions included which questions to ask their informants and how to capture their dialects[1]. Although it may be hard to understand, it is necessary to tell the whole story.

I implore anyone who has not explored this amazing historical project and the remarkable individuals who kept it alive, to take a moment to visit the Library of Congress's online database of photographs, folklore, and other records in the public archives.

Sources and Books for Continued Reading

[1] Library of Congress. *Born in Slavery: Slave Narratives from the Federal Writers' Project, 1936–1938*. Washington, DC: Library of Congress.

The Negro in Virginia, by the Virginia Writers' Project, 1994

Lay My Burden Down: A Folk History of Slavery, edited by B. A. Botkin, 1945

Voices from Slavery: 100 Authentic Slave Narratives, edited by Norman R. Yetman, 1970

These Are Our Lives, published by the University of North Carolina Press, 1939

ACKNOWLEDGEMENTS

I give all thanks and praise to God for His guidance, strength, and inspiration throughout this journey. Without Him, this book would not have been possible.

To my dad, who passed away during my journey of writing this novel, I want to dedicate this book to you, too. Thank you for always loving me. You taught me how to be strong, resilient, and above all else, educated. You never saw me the way I saw myself, and I will always love you, no matter how others saw you. You're forever in my heart, Chops.

To my mom, thank you for being eager to read my work and for giving me your support. Your love for reading and history has been such an inspiration in my life. Thank you for paving the way. I love you.

To my wonderful husband, Damien, I couldn't have asked for a better partner to share my life with. Thank you for always believing in me and for pushing me to step out of my comfort zone. You're determined every day not to let my self-sabotaging win. You always find a way to remind me that I'm loved and more than average. Your love is unconditional and I thank God you chose me as your wife.

To my two beautiful grandmothers, Jean and Lucinda. I wish we had had more time together. I wish I'd gotten to know you both and learned everything you experienced, to teach me more about how to navigate this thing called life. Having both of you beside me during this process would've been monumental. I can only imagine the stories you had to share and the love that only a grandmother can give.

To my editing team, thank you for your amazing work and professionalism. You all assisted at different stages of the process, and each time gave me important feedback to help make this novel come to life. I wish each of you much success in your career!

To my beta readers, Wenda T., Marsalla K., Mary H., Jennell B., Alyx R., and Tamu M., thank you for your support and kind words. It makes it easier to know that you have friends and even people you've just met cheering you on. Thank you for taking the time to read these pages and give me your honest feedback. Time is precious, and I don't take for granted that you chose to spend it helping me.

Thank you to my friends and family who played a part in this process, whether with a word of encouragement, a shoulder to cry on, or a helping hand. Your presence in my life has made this journey not only possible but profoundly meaningful.

ABOUT THE AUTHOR

Elizabeth Ray is a contemporary literary fiction author with a passion for writing heartfelt stories centered on family, identity, and emotional healing. Originally from Woodbridge, Virginia, she now resides in Richmond with her husband and son. She holds a degree in English with a minor in African American Studies. When not writing, she enjoys spending time with family and friends and traveling around the world. *The Weight of Forgiveness* is her debut novel.

Instagram: @elizabethray_theauthor
www.elizabethraywrites.com

www.ingramcontent.com/pod-product-compliance
Lightning Source LLC
LaVergne TN
LVHW100528110826
845146LV00002B/817

* 9 7 9 8 2 1 8 5 9 3 5 2 0 *